Backwards and Forwards

Maggie Fogarty

THANKS:

A big thank you to my test readers, Pip Toms, Spencer Smart, and Sue Kittow. Your honest feedback was much appreciated.

And an extra big thanks to Spencer for the cover design and to Paul Weall for his help with the book formatting.

Finally, I'd like to thank our cockapoo dog Bonnie for dragging me away from the computer and out for walkies!

Maggie Fogarty

March 1976...

The thing I remember most is the rose covered wallpaper. Deep red roses against the palest of pink backgrounds. The designer must have had a thing about orderliness and symmetry. Every rose in its place, like soldiers lined up on a parade ground. Left right, left right, every gap the same as the last one.

I hated that paper, the garish roses peering out like overly made up women, 'no better than they ought to be' as my granny would say.

Is that what she'd say about me now?

Whenever I needed help with sleeping, and it was most nights in that place, I'd start to count those damn flowers starting at the bottom left, heading upwards and then back down again. By the time I'd got to 100, I could feel the effect. A dulling of the senses, slowed breathing, heavy eyelids.

Never mind sleeping pills. Military style roses worked every time and when I left, I even tore off a bit for safe keeping. Not that it survived more than a few months but in my head I can conjure up the pattern at will, wondering about the man – and surely it had to be a man – who decided that flowers and military precision have something in common.

'That place' as I still call it. St Brigid's Mother and Baby Home, or the facility for 'fallen women' as the older generation still referred it back then. 'Times were a changing' the mid 1960s beat poets had told us, but a decade later on the outskirts of the Cornish seaside town of Penzance, you'd never guess it. Here it might as well have been the 1950s, all buttoned up and ready to pass judgement on anyone who stepped off the path to moral righteousness. I'd certainly done that all right, not so much veering off the path as leaping from it with a vengeance.

Certainly no better than I ought to be.

Actually St Brigid's wasn't all that bad. By the mid 1970s, most of the nuns had been replaced by social workers and a good number of them were only a few years older than myself. Some were University students, on placements from their training courses and in another world that could have been me. I'd done better in my school O Level exams than expected, and was poised to go on to do A levels. Not that any of that mattered now.

I was 16 when I came to St Brigid's, already seven months pregnant and working as a receptionist at a hotel in St Ives. I'd escaped from my home in a Midlands village, telling my parents that I wanted to take a year out before committing to A levels. They weren't happy but accepted that they couldn't force me to stay on at school. Little did they know that I was expecting a baby, conceived when I had a brief fling with a local nightclub disc jockey, 'Mr DJ' as he was known back then. Actually it was more of a love affair – at least that's how I saw it – and I was devastated when he took off to Manchester, to another world and doubtless another girl. Of course he'd no idea about the pregnancy and I made sure it stayed that way. This was something I had to deal with myself, the one and only.

It was pretty easy to hide the pregnancy at first and I made sure I got a job a good few hundred miles away from home. No mobile phones or Skype calls in those days and no social media. A girl could go into hiding with the minimum of fuss and fashionable 'gypsy' style loose dresses hid my emerging bump.

Then the big give away, fainting one day after my boss put me on the breakfast serving rota. Someone hadn't turned up for work and it was all hands to the pump. I was already feeling queasy but the smell of fried food and the sight of runny eggs tipped me over the edge. One minute I was making polite conversation with a genial visitor and the next, bang. Flat out on the dining room floor, only to wake up with a crowd of people around me with someone mouthing that a doctor was on the way.

No hiding things now. It didn't take long for the medic to suss out why I'd fainted and she slipped me the telephone number of St Brigid's. Realising the game was over, I handed in my notice and made my way on the bus to Penzance, all the time willing myself not to throw up.

A young social worker met me at the station and although she tried to be friendly on the drive to the home, we both knew where this was leading. I'd be there for a couple of months, have the baby and then after a few weeks would hand it over to one of the many families waiting to adopt.

St Brigid's served its purpose, a gateway for those with unwanted pregnancies to provide for those who desperately needed their own child. If this was one of those gritty TV dramas, I'd be the poor victim forced to give up her child to a rich couple who could give it a better life. I'd be suitably distraught, watching my child being driven away while I wanted to hang on to it with every bone in my body.

Except it wasn't like that. At the time I felt strangely disconnected from the little human being growing inside me, wanting it to be out in the world and spirited away. One of the social workers told me that I was 'in denial' and that I needed to be prepared to feel differently when I did have the baby. 'That's why we leave things for a while, to see if you change your mind' she added, convinced that she was right.

She was wrong of course. When 7lbs. 9oz. Edward arrived quickly on a windy March day in 1976, I felt nothing but an overwhelming sense of relief. Glad that this would be all over soon and that I could go back to being a ditzy 16 year old again. Glad that I didn't have to tell my mum and dad that they were grandparents and that my sister had a much younger nephew.

Sorry if it sounds hard, but that's the truth. It was only a long time afterwards, decades down the line, that things changed. At the time I handed over Edward with the minimum of fuss, reassuring the social workers that yes, I really did know what I was doing.

There was no father named on the birth certificate, after I told St Brigid's that my pregnancy was the result of a drunken tryst at a house party. And that was that. Edward off to a lovely couple from up North and me free to decide what to do with the rest of my life.

Nice, neat and orderly. Just like those roses on my St Brigid's home wallpaper.

Except life is never that simple and mine is no exception. That's why I'm here today on the outskirts of Penzance, on the site of St Brigid's, now a swanky Spa hotel and trendy retreat.

Waiting for my teenage daughter Amy to arrive.

Preparing to tell her the truth about her mother's past and a half-brother she knows nothing about.

Chapter One

There's nothing left of the old St Brigid's building, the only nods to its past being a few faded photographs on the reception wall.

Originally an isolation hospital, it became a mother and baby home in the 1950s, then run by a combination of nuns and supporting residential staff. Most of the photographs are from the 1950s and 1960s, and by the look of things little had altered by time I arrived over a decade later.

Today, the uber trendy Kernow Spa Hotel stands where St Brigid's once was. A modern, airy building bathed in plenty of light and styled in a chic minimalist fashion, with lots of pale blues and greys. It's smart enough to have featured in a number of Sunday magazine supplements, with one of the big attractions being the wedding packages. Looking out across the expansive grounds you can appreciate why and already I can see that a marquee has been put up in readiness for a marriage celebration.

Of course, my daughter Amy knows nothing of my former association with this place. In fact she's unaware of a big chunk of my early life, including the fact that she has an adopted half-brother living in Canada.

A brother who nearly 40 years ago was born on this very spot to a confused and frightened teenage mum.

To help clear my head, I'm wandering around the pristine gardens but there is no sense of familiarity. Not that I did much exploring all those years ago, pretty much locking myself in my room, willing the days to pass until I could escape and start my life over. I remember one girl called Susan who I'd chat to from time to time, a sweet natured local who had got in the family way after meeting a young mixed race guy down on holiday from Sheffield. While he was prepared to 'do the right thing' and marry her, Susan's parents would have none of it. Aged just 17, she was dispatched to St Brigid's to have what her parents called 'that black bastard baby' and told not to say anything to friends or other family. Shocking by today's standards but not unheard of back then.

I never did find out what happened to poor Susan. Unlike me, she had bonded straight away with her baby and fought to keep it right up to the end. It was a battle she didn't win though and coming back here has made me wonder what happened to her over the years. I have only a vague recollection of how she looked but I remember those haunted eyes when she came to say goodbye. Rarely have I seen such deep sadness and resignation in someone so young.

But back to the here and now, the place I really

need to be. Amy is travelling over from London tomorrow and was bemused when I suggested that we meet here.

'But why go for a hotel so close to home?' she asked me when I gave the address and contact number.

'Because it will do us good to be on a neutral territory and you'll find out soon enough why.'

She waited a few moments before answering, weighing up my words suspiciously.

'Hmm it all seems a bit fishy to me. Then again, nothing should surprise me about your behaviour lately.'

Ouch. That had been meant to hurt and Amy knew it. I bit my lip and decided to ignore her barbed comment. There will be much more where that came from once we start talking for real, a hell of a lot more.

Right now I'm mentally trying to recreate the layout of the original grounds, the granite stone buildings which had looked so menacing when I first arrived, clutching my small suitcase and the remains of a packed lunch. The gardens didn't seem as spacious back then, perhaps because the home loomed large, casting its dark shadow across the landscape. Today the sun is out and jaunty flower beds border the carefully manicured lawns. It's pretty and welcoming, just as a popular Cornish wedding venue should be.

I wonder how many of the couples choosing this

place to take their vows, know about its gloomy history? Not many I suspect and if they do, then what the hell? Times have changed and even old prisons with their grim toll of hangings and torture, are turned into trendy hotels or restaurants these days.

....

Amy is due to arrive here soon and our reunion is going to be awkward to put it mildly. I haven't seen her since she stormed out of the house over a week ago, livid that I'd covered up her dead father's affair. Even now I can barely bring myself to say those words.

Dead. Father. Affair. Such an ugly combination but true.

'Take things carefully. Remember one step at a time. Don't overload her with stuff.' Sage advice given from Kevin Foster my best friend, work colleague, and now live-in lover.

Kevin isn't at all keen on my choice of venue – 'it feels a bit sick to be honest Debbie' – but he does understand the need for me to be alone with Amy away from the day to day distractions of home and work. Poor Kevin, what he has had to put up with since he moved in with us less than a year ago. Good job we knew each other well, friends before lovers and familiar work mates to boot.

As for Amy, she's already had to grow up quickly, my husband David dying just before her 16th birthday, exactly the same age I gave birth here to her half brother. Hell, how am I going to bring that into the conversation, once I've got the sordid story of David's betrayal out of the way?

My thoughts are interrupted by a sudden blast of 'Canon in D Major' by Pachelbel, coming from the direction of the wedding marquee. Clearly they are testing the sound system, trying to make sure that there will be no hiccups on the big day. It's surprisingly moving and I can feel myself starting to well up. All that optimism and hope for the future, for family celebration and looking forward to a lifetime together. Isn't that what the stuff of weddings is all about?

Yet here I am about to reveal to my daughter a family history that will rock her already uncertain world.

Time now to go back inside, to prepare for the hardest conversation of my life so far.

Amy please find it in yourself to forgive, to understand that everything I have done has been for good reasons.

For better or worse.

Chapter 2

Over to me...Amy talking.

My turn to speak up now. It's me, little ol' Amy, that awkward kick-ass runaway daughter on her way back to Cornwall after a week's stay in London. Actually 'retreat' would be a better description as I was hiding away from the world in my own little bubble.

At least I don't have to travel straight home to Truro, as for some odd reason mum wants to meet up in a swanky hotel on the edge of Penzance. She's been behaving strangely of late has mum. My boyfriend Ashley thinks it's all down to the menopause. 'Women can go a bit odd at that time of life' he told me, with the tone of one of those popular newspaper advice doctors.

Except mum hasn't shown any signs of 'oddness' before now. In fact she's a pretty fit looking fifty something, with a nice figure and a new younger boyfriend. She's got a cool job too as a writer and events manager on a Cornish magazine and has a real dude of a boss. Yes, she seems to be embracing middle age and thriving on it. Still, Ashley could be right, I guess.

I mean, how else am I supposed to read her behaviour of late? First she seems to think that I've got some kind of weird fixation with her hot shot boss Carl Martin. Come on. He's fun and fit but that's the end of it. Just because we had a bit of playful banter during my work experience stint at the magazine, doesn't mean jack shit. Our generation can just be friends you know and it doesn't all have to be about sex.

Then there was the disgusting way that I found out what my dad had been up to before he died. And how? During a casual meeting with a young woman called Jemma, who just happened to have been my dad's mistress. That's bloody how. It didn't take me long to put two and two together, realising that mum must have already known. She'd even told her boyfriend Kevin but thought it best to keep me, her own flesh and blood, in the dark.

Let's face it, who wouldn't be angry about uncovering a grubby family secret like that? Dad was my bloody hero, the man I looked up to and I wanted somebody just like him for my own future husband.

So to discover that he'd been sneaking behind our backs, living in another flat with a woman not that much older than me, was not only a slap in the face but a grenade tossed into the heart of my cherished memories of him.

Fondly remembered dad, David, morphed into

philanderer, cheat, liar. Mum not that much better either, letting me find out the way I did. Feeling sorry for myself? Yeah, too right I am.

Still, those few days in London have done me good and I've made a big decision. The time is right to take a year out of university to go travelling and Ashley's coming with me. Mum will be livid but you know what? It's my life and I need to take control. The study can wait for a bit and given what she's done, mum can hardly complain. I mean she left home when she was only sixteen and I'm a whole three years older. Besides, I'm pretty grown up for my age as mum well knows.

The decision has made me feel a whole lot better. Dad would have been fuming too, and although he's no longer around, it's my way of getting back at him.

It's not long now until the train gets into Penzance and then a short taxi ride to the hotel. Truth is, I'm a bit less angry with mum than I was, but I still need to play the hurt daughter role before letting her know about my plans to go off travelling.

Hand on heart though, I'm starting to get a tad nervous about telling her - after all, for good or ill, she's still my mum. To be fair, and if she's telling me the truth, she only found out about dad's affair a few months back and believed she was protecting his memory by keeping it from me. Lies are always worse though, aren't they? Sooner or later I was bound to find out – the young woman Jemma was even still living in our home city of Truro – so it would have been better all round if mum had bitten the bullet and told me.

The sea looks stunning as we edge our way through Marazion and Long Rock towards Penzance. I've loved my time in London but on a sunny day, it's hard to beat Cornwall and despite everything, it's good to be back.

'Where you heading then?' the taxi driver asks, as he loads my bags into the car boot.

'Kernow Spa hotel' I reply, in no mood for a friendly chat.

'Fancy place that – are you celebrating something?'

Ha, bloody ha.

'Not really. Just meeting my mum.'

To my relief he gets distracted by a radio call while I make a point of checking my texts. It usually shuts people up and there's one that's just popped up from Ashley.

'Hi – hope it all goes well with your mum. Ring me later babe, love you loads. xx'

Stay focused Amy. Remember, it's you that's been wronged and mum has some explaining to do.

This time around I want to know bloody everything, lock stock and barrel.

Chapter 3

Back to yours truly, Debbie McKay....

Right now I'm perched in the hotel bar and waiting for Amy to make her entrance. I already know she's on the way because I've had a terse text to say so, with none of the usual 'love Amy', kisses or emoticons. Just a blunt 'in taxi now, see you soon.'

I want the old affectionate Amy back, not this business like stranger, texting as if she's on her way to meet a colleague rather than her mum. Despite my better judgement, I've ordered a large chilled white wine. Having just got off the phone to my lovely 'other half' Kevin, his words are still ringing out.

'Keep a clear brain Debbie and stay off the booze. You don't want to be getting all over emotional.'

Sorry Kevin but no can do. This vino crutch is needed to calm my nerves, so being sensible has to take a back seat. There's a hell of a roller coaster ride looming ahead and I've never been one for fairground attractions. Having only been on one of those 'big dipper' rides once, I threw up and swore never to go near one again.

On that score at least, I've stayed true to my word.

About ten minutes to go then before Amy gets here. Just enough time to down my wine and replace it with a glass of water.

Here's the plan, such as it is. After all the niceties and the apologies – trust me there will be both – I'll start with why I chose to keep the discovery of her deceased dad's affair hidden from her. The hardest bit will be explaining why I'd already shared the news with Kevin but I think I can deal with that. She's bound to ask more questions about the mistress Jemma, and I'll tell her again what I know. Which actually doesn't amount to much at this stage.

There will be nothing said this evening about her adopted half-brother Andy. That can wait until tomorrow and there will be no easy way of telling the story. By comparison, the revelation of her dad's betrayal will more straightforward, a brewing storm before the full force hurricane.

A great believer in 'positive visualisation' – painting a good outcome scene for every occasion – it's difficult to create a cheery image for either conversation, however hard I try. In an ideal happy clappy world, Amy would come over all forgiving and tell me how she understood the need to protect her dad's memory, to shield her from the unsavoury details. Then she'd greet the news of her half-brother with a mixture of tearful surprise followed by delight. Tears followed by smiles and all would be well with the world again.

As if.

No, try as I might, this neatly packaged response to my news isn't going to happen. You can create all the text book positivity you like, but the real world will chuck back a big dollop of down and dirty realism.

About five minutes to go and I'm staring into my compact mirror of all things, checking that my lipstick is still in place. Displacement activity for sure and my eyes are showing the effects of a week's lack of sleep, all puffy with flecks of red.

'Would you like another drink?' the bar assistant cuts in, glancing at my empty glass.

'Just a water please' I reply, shuffling the lipstick stained vessel across the counter.

I'm beginning to regret ignoring the advice of make-up professionals to go for the eyes or lips, but not both. No time now though to do anything about it.

As the taxi pulls up outside, I can see Amy hovering while driver opens the car boot to unload her bags. She's looking beautiful, quite serene even.

Sensing my awkwardness, the bar assistant gently places my glass of water on the table, giving a reassuring smile. I return it with all the authenticity of a cheap wig - it's a damn fake and we both know it.

Spotting me from a distance, Amy gives a perfunctory wave but no smile. Here we go then, no turning back, the beginning of the rest of our lives careering in the direction of God only knows where.

Chapter 4

I just want to hug Amy, to tell her how much I love her and to go back to our old easy relationship. She probably wants that too, but instead we are facing each other like two awkward strangers, neither one of us knowing where to begin.

'Did you have a good journey?' Jeez, is this really what I'm asking my daughter? As if to apologise for my crassness, I reach out to touch her arm. She flinches, tugging at her suitcase.

'The journey was fine. Let me get these bags out of the way.' Before I have a chance to react, she's off in the direction of the reception area, leaving me standing like a 'prize prat' as Kevin would describe it.

It is probably only a few minutes, but it seems an age before Amy gets back.

'Sorry about that. I needed to have a pee as well – I hate using train toilets.'

I'm smiling now, still trying to break the ice, but Amy is having none of it.

'What are you drinking?' she asks, eyeing up my full glass.

'Well it's not a vodka and tonic, just fizzy water.' Again I'm trying to be upbeat, offering to buy her a drink or even a bite to eat.

'Thanks, just a cranberry juice for now.' She's still not making proper eye contact, instead focussing somewhere in the middle distance.

As I head over to order the drink, I see that she's checking out her phone, probably looking to see if there are any messages from her beau Ashley.

'I'll bring it across if you like' the bar assistant offers but I tell her that its fine, I'll take it myself. Again, displacement activity but it gives Amy a few minutes to settle.

Drinks now in place, where to start?

'Amy, before we have our proper chat, how was London?' My mind is flitting back to the last time I was there, when I met my son Andy, forty years after giving him away. Both of my children ending up with first names beginning with 'A'. Funny how that turned out.

Amy is looking straight at me now, the first time she has made proper eye contact since arriving.

'You look knackered, have you not been sleeping?' If I'm not imagining it, there's a hint of sympathy, so all is not lost then.

'Not much, I've been worrying about you. Anyway, tell me about London.'

'There's not much to tell. The apartment is lovely, right on the South Bank but me and Ashley didn't go out much. We just chilled out in his dad's swanky place, watching films and getting take-out meals.'

It's lovely just to hear her voice, so I stay silent, hoping that she'll talk a bit more.

'Anyway, let's not waste time on London. I want to hear more about Jemma and dad...' Amy has been quick to spot my ruse to put off the big conversation.

'OK Amy, point taken but let's find somewhere a bit more quiet. Why don't we head outside and take advantage of the warm evening?'

We find a table at the far end of the terrace, overlooking the pristine lawn and the marquee.

'That's for a wedding over the weekend' I explain as we take our seats.

'Must be a posh one' Amy replies, taking in the size of the marquee and the stack of tables placed neatly alongside it.

'I expect so. This place doesn't come cheap.' And indeed it doesn't. All in, this little heart-to-heart with my daughter is costing the price of a week's break on the continent. Sorry Kevin, but that promised romantic get-away will have to wait for a while.

'So why have you chosen here then? We could just as well talk at home.'

She'll soon know the significance all right, but not just yet.

'I thought it best that we get away from things for a bit, perhaps even have a few spa treatments ...'

'Mum, we're not here on a girly break remember? Stop trying to change the subject – Jemma and dad. OK?'

I'm trying to keep my patience, I really am. But this version of my daughter is starting to get on my nerves.

'Yes I know what we're here for and bloody well ditch that snotty tone of voice.' As I say the words, I'm immediately regretting them but hell I'm tired and she's being a surly little madam.

My snapping at her has its effect and there's a sudden change of body language. Within seconds Amy has morphed from bad tempered cow to a six year old being told off by mum.

'Sorry Amy but I'm – as you just put it – knackered and no I've not forgotten what we're here for. Hell I've thought about nothing else for the past week.'

'I know that mum but I just want to know what's been going on.' There's a flash of a conciliatory smile, something to be hopeful about.

'Right then, here's what I've found out so far about Jemma and your dad, no holds barred.'

'Mum just let me ask the questions first and then you can answer.'

She wants to be in control, to steer the conversation. And how can I refuse?

'Fine. We'll do it your way then.' I take a large gulp of water, waiting for the first one.

'When exactly did you find out mum?'

Suddenly, I'm thrown back into my little kitchen back in Truro, the clock ticking louder than I've ever heard it before. Jemma's selection of birthday and valentine cards, intimate notes, strewn across the table. All of them addressed to my husband of over 25 years. My now deceased husband and father to Amy.

A deep intake of breath.

'It was on a Saturday afternoon at 3.15pm, when I opened that envelope.'

Chapter 5

Once back in the moment so to speak, there's no stopping me. Amy stays quiet, listening intently, any planned questions on the back burner for now.

I can quote those damn cards word for word, so no need for copies. Having left the originals with Jemma – returning her filthy lost property – I made no attempt to do duplicates beforehand. Short of getting severe memory problems, her messages to my husband will stay with me to my grave.

True to my promise, I do little to spare Amy. One of the messages is cringe inducing in its gushing tribute to my husband's prowess in bed.

'Dave last night was amazing, you are a great teacher and me the willing pupil. Older men definitely have their advantages! I can't concentrate on work today just thinking about your body, hands, everything babe. Roll on next Tuesday but I've got plenty of fantasies to be going on with. Lots of love and lust. xx'

Of course I've only given Amy the gist here, after all it's her dead father we are talking about for heaven's sake. Still, I can see the hurt – and disgust – on her face and it's killing me to watch.

Breaking the silence, Amy spits out the reference to 'Dave.'

'Ugh, dad used to say he hated abbreviated names. That's why mine is so short. God it sounds so cheesy and she writes like a besotted 14 year old....' She breaks off to take a large sip of her drink but there is no hiding the pain.

I wait a few seconds before continuing.

'A few hours after I found all this stuff, I was due to go out for drinks with my editor Elaine. I nearly called it off but I'm glad I didn't...'

Cue to say how I blurted out everything to Elaine and then the shock news that she actually knew this Jemma woman. The little strumpet – yes I'm back in that angry stage again – had even once worked on Cornwall Now magazine as a marketing intern. With me being freelance, I'd had no idea. Elaine had then gone on to give her a glowing reference for a job on the Echo newspaper, the one where David worked as head of sales. The rest, as they say, is history.

Amy's face has reddened, her expression changing from hurt to anger.

'So Elaine was the very first person you told and not Kevin. With me, your own flesh and blood, the last in the queue. Frigging hell mum you are unbelievable.'

She's right of course, with the benefit of hindsight. But I mustn't bite back, simply take things on the chin and try to move forwards.

'All right Amy, it was wrong not to tell you. Think about it though, you were at University, about to take important exams and you had more than enough on your plate.'

For some reason, she winces at my mention of university, as if I've reminded her of a safer more innocent world. A protective bubble before the precious memories of her dad imploded.

'Look I didn't want you upset, to distract you from your studies. Kevin agreed that it was best to keep this under wraps.'

Amy's reverted back to her indignant look, smarting at the mention of Kevin.

'And you listened to him? Mum we never have – I mean had – secrets. Anyway, I was bound to find out somewhere along the line.'

To be fair to her, I hadn't really given this possibility much thought. Amy was studying in Bristol for most of the year and if it wasn't for me setting up her work experience at Cornwall Now, I doubt whether their paths would ever have crossed. More fool me for ignoring my gut instinct about mixing work with family.

'Amy I honestly didn't expect you to meet Jemma. Stupid I know. Kevin and me just thought it best that you remembered your dad for who he was most of the time – not just for the last year or so of his life.'

She's staring hard at me now, hands clenched around her glass and biting her bottom lip. Then the slap of cold liquid on my chest, the slivers of ice cascading across the ground.

'Amy what the hell..?'

She's up and off before I can finish my sentence, cranberry juice running down the front of my sheer white blouse, like watered down blood. I grab hold of a napkin but the damage is done.

Thank God we are the only ones sitting outside. Clutching the sodden napkin, I head back to the bar area but there's no sign of Amy.

'If you're looking for your friend, she went that way' the bar assistant says, staring at the stain on my blouse.

'Oh thanks – just had a bit of an accident with my drink.'

Before we can get into any discussion about why and how, I make a sharp exit towards the toilet facilities to see if I can make myself a bit more respectable. Starting to run the warm tap, I can hear low level sobs coming from one of the cubicles.

'Amy – is that you in there?'

And as the sobs grow louder, I have my answer. Of course it's her and right now she needs her mum.

'Come on, it's only a damn blouse. Let's get me tidied up and we'll start again. OK?'

Silence then the slow opening of the cubicle door. No words are needed, just the two of us holding each other tight.

For now at least, I have my daughter where she belongs.

Chapter 6

We're back on the hotel terrace, no sign anymore of the scattered ice and discarded glass. Another couple have come to sit outside, cooing over the view across the hotel grounds.

It's early evening but the sun is still out and we move to another table to keep a decent distance between ourselves and the transfixed middle aged couple.

Strangely, it feels safer having someone else around, a guarantee of sorts that there won't be a repeat of the ice throwing incident. For that Amy did have the grace to apologise, red faced and stuttering.

We've left out the drinks this time, Amy even managing a joke that it is better to be safe than sorry.

'Why didn't you copy those cards from Jemma?' she asks, after we've settled into our seats. Whoa, straight back to the nitty-gritty then.

'Because I told you they are still in my head. Word for word. Believe me, that is more than enough to cope with without having the physical copies.'

'And this flat over in St Agnes dad got hold of. Have you been to see it?'

The news of the flat had come as another huge shock to me, revealed during my face-to-face meeting with mistress Jemma. Trust me, I'd thought about going over there, to get a look at their sordid little hideaway. Kevin though, was cautious and didn't see the point of me torturing myself any more. Still, Amy has a point.

'No not yet.' See I've left the door open for the possibility.

'Think you should and I'd like to see the place too.'

Hmm. Something to be negotiated.

'Let's park that one for now Amy. I haven't even got the address.'

A flicker of irritation passes across her face.

'Well mum I've still got Jemma's details and if you don't arrange something, I will.'

'I didn't say I wouldn't, just that it's not the right time - yet.'

That seems to do the trick with just a slight pause before the next question comes my way.

'So was this the real deal for them? Or was dad, you know, just doing that middle aged thing of chancing his luck with a younger woman?'

From what I understand, Jemma certainly believed it was the genuine thing. They'd been planning a holiday and he thought enough about her to set up a little love nest, somewhere they could cosy up on the weekends when he was supposed to be working away.

Still, how am I to second guess what was going through his mind? Was he really prepared to throw away 25 years of marriage and his relationship with Amy? We'll never find out for sure, whatever Jemma thinks is the case.

'Jemma told me that their relationship was serious and you don't have a fling for more than a year or go to the trouble he did to hide it.'

'You know mum, you don't even seem that angry anymore, or is it just an act?' I can see Amy is staring across at my wedding ring which yes, I still haven't psyched myself up to remove.

'I was bloody fuming when I first found out. Screaming inside, crazy angry. If he'd still been around, there'd be no accounting for my actions.'

Another silence, Amy glancing across at the middle aged couple who are ordering a bottle of bubbly. Their celebratory mood is at odds with our own feelings of revulsion and betrayal.

'Wonder what their happy occasion is?' I ask, thinking out loud.

Amy ignores my question, her eyes fixed back on my wedding ring.

'Why are you still wearing that then?'

I have no real answer, other than despite

everything, I can't turn my love for David off like a tap.

'Habit I suppose' is my glib reply.

Amy sniffs, shuffling in her seat.

'Yeah I guess that is what we really were to dad. A habit, something he got bored with.'

Her words are harsh, but directed at him more than me. She could be right. Perhaps all David wanted was an escape route from the humdrum nature of every day family life.

'Let's face it mum, he can't have loved us. Not really. If you love someone, you don't crawl behind their backs, living a lie with someone else.'

I can see that she is on the verge of tears and reach across to give her hand a reassuring squeeze. This time she doesn't pull back from physical contact, a sign that I've broken through the anger directed at me.

Small mercies, except it doesn't last for long.

'And you know what still really hurts mum? What dad did was disgusting, vile but what you did was almost as bad. Not telling me something like that, yet sharing it with Elaine and Kevin. I don't think I'll ever recover from the way I found out.'

The tears are streaming down thick and fast,

Not from Amy. It's me crying now, unable to stop myself.

Across the terrace, a champagne cork is popped,

followed by the cheerful clinking of glasses.

Laughter and happiness, paired with venom and tears. The stuff of everyday family life you might say.

Well, some family this is turning out to be, the stuff of those terrible daytime confession TV shows, the ones where they whip out lie detectors to see who is telling the truth.

Except this isn't just a TV episode to gawk and sneer at. This is our real life story unfolding here and there's still a lot more at stake.

Chapter 7

'Let's take a walk in the grounds' I suggest, as we leave behind the joyful couple to drink their champagne alone on the terrace.

'I can't get my head around why you've picked this place.' Amy is first to break our silence, aware that I'm still upset, eyes now even more swollen and reddened.

Despite everything, I've got to stick with the original plan. First, deal with David's affair and the rest - that really big stuff – can wait. The true significance of this location will then be unveiled.

'Promise, I'll put you in the picture tomorrow and anyway, I thought it was you who wanted to stick to the subject of your dad.'

'OK but while we're on that, can I expect any kind of apology for how you hid this from me?'

Again, it's a fair question. Even if it was done with the best of intentions, the consequences have been appalling. So it's a case of damn well biting the bullet.

'I'm sorry Amy. I truly am. You should never have found out the way you did and I ought to have thought things through more.'

I wait as Amy absorbs my words, her expression neutral.

'Well, that's something I suppose but it's going to take time for me to trust you mum. You'll have to put up with that.'

'I know darling and I'm not going to keep things from you again.'

We are both walking briskly, heads down, body language stiff.

The wedding marquee looms ahead, the true scale of it more apparent as we approach.

'Tell me about your and dad's wedding' Amy says, her off beam question taking me aback. It suddenly occurs that I've never told my daughter about our wedding and to be fair, up until this point, she's never asked. Of course, she's seen the photos, me in a shoulder padded red striped 1980s dress, with a then fashionable spiky haircut. David in a navy blue suit, the only one he had, with a thin matching leather tie. We were both in our early twenties, the world at our feet and ridiculously in love. What could go wrong?

Amy is waiting for me to respond, giving a sideways glance to gauge my reaction. She looks surprised to see me smiling.

'There's not much to tell really, it wasn't a big deal like this one. We didn't have a lot of money so sloped off to the Registry Office and then had a few days in a hotel in Jersey.'

'Ah, so it wasn't this one then?' Amy is still trying to second guess why we are here.

'No but it was lovely and for us, a bit of luxury.' I don't add that we barely got out of bed, ordering room service when the mood took us. Too much information, as the saying goes.

'And no other family there on the wedding day either....just you and dad?'

'We did have some friends as witnesses, a couple of work mates, and they are on a few of the photos. Don't forget that your grandad was ill then and couldn't travel to Cornwall.'

Another long pause, our walking pace quickening.

'When I get married I want a big wedding, with all my friends and family there. A bit like this one, no expense spared.' Amy is looking again at the marquee, with its stack of satin backed chairs, a pile of pink bows waiting to be fitted to the backs.

'You'd better get saving then' I quip, before remembering that her boyfriend Ashley is from a wealthy family. If he is truly future husband material, Amy will no doubt get the wedding she wants.

'Hmm. Anyway mum I've got some news for you and be prepared - you aren't going to like it.'

Oh Lord. Already I'm steeling myself for what is coming next. Please God she's not pregnant and what a terrible irony that would be, right here of all places.

Amy stops and takes a deep breath, turning to face me head on.

'Look, Ashley and me have been chatting a lot over the past few days, about life, how it can leave you reeling, feeling like shit. Like finding out about dad. Anyway, it's made us decide to do something drastic, seize the day while we can.'

We're staring directly at each other while I wait to hear more.

'And? Go on Amy...'

Another intake of breath, this time from me.

'We're leaving uni and don't start kicking off because it's not for ever, just taking a year out. To travel, see some of the world...'

Hell, I can barely believe what I'm hearing. Amy, who was so looking forward to university and is having the time of her life. Or so I believed.

'And before you say anything else mum, our minds are made up. We can pick up on our studies the year after we get back, I've already spoken to my tutor...'

I've now grabbed hold of Amy's arm and she winces as I tighten my grip.

'Now listen here, you can't just go off like that – is it Ashley who has put this idiotic idea into your head?'

'Let go of my arm mum you're hurting.'

I release her arm, furious that she's about to do something that could ruin her future. Will she really want to return to university after a year of travelling? No bones about it, this is Ashley's fault all right. A rich boy who doesn't need to work for a living, cushioned as he is with privilege and family money.

'No, don't you go blaming everything on Ashley. This is my idea. My way of coping with the shock over dad. I need time out to get a sense of perspective. It's only for a year...'

Oh yeah, sure it is. A year of living it up on Ashley's trust fund and she'll be running straight back to university. Like hell she will.

'Anyway, I'm old enough to make my own mind up, so stop trying to get me to do what you regret not doing yourself. You never even went to university and you've done OK for yourself.'

'Times have changed and you need a degree these days to get on. Anyway, why can't you wait until you've finished university?'

'Because mum I need the time off now.' Her voice is raised, arms folded defensively.

My mind has gone into over drive. Lord, this is like a bizarre game of family political ping pong, each player having to up their game. First I'm forced to apologise for not telling her about her dad's affair, then she hits back at me with the decision to leave her university course after just a year. Bat.

Ball. Ping. Pong.

And tomorrow, as they say, is another bloody day.

Chapter 8

Over to me again - Amy speaking...

It's me, Amy, alone this time and in the room next door to mum's. It's a lovely light room, if a bit on the small side after Ashley's dad's palatial apartment.

I can just about make out mum's voice through the wall. She's probably on the phone to Kevin, telling him how I'm about to destroy my life chances by taking a poxy year out. Jeez, anyone would think me and Ashley are leaving uni forever, the way she is banging on. Loads of people drop out for a year, either through illness, family death or whatever else you care to name. I mean come on, we've got our a whole life ahead of us, with plenty of time to pick up the pieces when we get back from travelling.

Mum's always moaning about how she wishes she had gone on to do a degree and my answer is always the same. What's stopping her? There's Open University and we've got quite a few oldies on my course, people who've been made redundant and want to go into a new profession, or who just want to study for the sake of it.

Yes she's busy with her work, but some of our older undergraduates still have jobs. Come to think of it, most of the people on my course have some kind of employment even in term time. I suppose I'm lucky that mum has given me enough of an allowance to make sure I don't have to go out to work and as for Ashley, well enough said. He's loaded after his gran left him a generous stash.

Still, I meant it when I said that I'm old enough to make up my own mind. Ashley's told his dad about our plans and he was supportive, suggesting that we spend some time at his home in Sydney. I'd love that but Ashley's already been there loads of times, so is less bothered. He's keener on places like America, Canada, the Far East. Just thinking about it makes my skin tingle with excitement.

Whatever mum thinks, there's no stopping us and Ashley's already started work on the itinerary, like the proverbial pig in muck.

Mum's voice seems to be getting louder, as if she's yelling down the phone. You can bet that poor Kevin is getting an ear bashing, with her taking it out on him. I've noticed that she's been doing a lot of that lately and Kevin just puts up with it. Occasionally, he'll defend himself against the onslaught but not often enough in my opinion. He needs to - what's the saying? - 'man up' more.

Anyway, the worst is over as far as I'm concerned. Don't get me wrong, I'm still fuming about dad – did you hear that up there dad? You are a prize prick, a saddo and you don't deserve our love. Are you listening wherever you are?

At least mum has apologised and she can't exactly tell me what to do after the disgraceful way she's behaved. My life, my choices. She did the same when she was younger, running away to Cornwall and never going back to her home in the Midlands, except for the occasional visit.

I remember my nan telling me that mum was a 'right handful' when she was growing up, always heading out to nightclubs and not coming in until the early hours. She said mum liked wearing mini skirts and high heels, with grandad telling her that she looked like a 'street walker'.

'You're a much more sensible girl than your mum was Amy' she told me, nodding with approval. So there you have it. Mum can hardly complain about me when she was such a rebel herself.

I have to admit that she did look devastated after I told her and despite everything, she's still my mum. Tell you what, I'll make it up to her later, try to be a bit nicer and offer to pay for dinner. Go back to my sweet daughter Amy role.

As for the rest of this evening? Head down to the restaurant about 7pm and carry on quizzing mum about Jemma and dad. I still have a good few questions and I want to pin her down about the two of us going over to see what was dad's secret love nest in St Agnes.

I also want us to meet up again with Jemma, the two of us together this time.

So that's the next few hours sorted.

Hang on, what the hell is that noise? It sounds like something has just crashed up against the wall.

Shit, what is mum up to now?

Chapter 9

Back to me - still fuming with that daughter of mine...

I'm supposed to be the grown-up, the parent and didn't plan to hurl the phone across the room. I mean the sensible, rational Debbie McKay, mum and professional woman, would never in a million years do something so childish.

Yet I've just done that very thing. Finished my call to Kevin and then hurled the hand set across the room, watching as it bounced off the edge of the table and then hit the wall. Predictably, Amy is now banging on the door wanting to know what the fuck is going on.

'Mum – are you OK? What was that noise?'

'It's fine Amy, the phone just slipped out of my hand and flicked against the wall.' True – more or less.

'It sounded pretty loud for a flick.' She's already doubting my story but heads back to her room when I yell back that yes, everything really is fine and dandy.

It's all down to Kevin that I lost my temper, with his patronising goody-goody 'I know best' attitude. First he told me off about drinking when I confessed to having a large glass of wine to help me face Amy.

'Debbie – you know what we said about you not drinking, keeping a clear head and all that.'

'Sanctimonious prick' were my unsaid words. Well he can be like that sometimes and it gets on my nerves.

Then he was ridiculously relaxed when I told him about Amy's plan to leave university and go travelling. I couldn't help myself, really I couldn't.

'Oh and I suppose you'd be fine if your two boys suddenly decided to up and leave their degree courses? Assuming they ever get there in the first place.'

As soon as the words tumbled out I regretted them. It wasn't fair to take out my anger on him. Amy isn't his daughter, damn it.

'Sorry I didn't mean it to come out like that Kevin...'

'I know you're upset Debbie and no, I wouldn't like it either if it were my boys. But she's an adult and has promised to go back after a year.'

I'm biting my lip hard. That blood drawing, painful sort of hard. Trying not to say how naive he is to think that is ever likely to happen. Come on, once she's got the taste for Ashley's high living life style, then that will be it. No degree, professional plans tossed away.

'She might go back but then again Kevin – I mean why such a rush to travel anyway?'

His long pause says it all. Back off Debbie or you'll just make things much worse. Don't be over dramatic, stop over-thinking it. In other words lighten up.

'Well the way I see it Debbie you got no choice. If you try to stop them it will just make things much worse and – forgive me for saying this – Amy has had a lot to deal with lately.'

'Ah, so this is my fault then Kevin? Is that what you really think?'

What do they say about the red mist of anger? This one is a vivid scarlet, right bang in the middle of my head.

He gives one of those resigned sighs, the ones that mean 'I give up.' His message couldn't be clearer. Deal with your own family mess and don't dump it on me.

'Listen here Debbie I didn't say it was your fault and if you're going to be like that, we should stop talking right now.' Then the loud click that said it all, over and out.

That's when I launched my phone into the air, the crash louder than expected. Shit. I hope it has survived the impact.

With Amy appeased, a quick inspection of the outer casing shows that it's more robust than it looks. There's an ugly scratch along the front where it hit the corner of the table and only a slight dent in the wall where it made contact.

Kevin's number is the last one I rang but I'm hardly going to call him back just to see if the phone is still working. The number before Kevin's is for Philippe Roux, the lovely veterinary guy I met on my recent visit to Canada. That first time visit to meet my adopted son's family.

Philippe is one of those people you can open up to. Although he's a scientist, an expert in small animal surgery, he is good with people. Come to think of it, most of the people I know who work with animals have a knack with humans too. It must come with the territory.

It will be early afternoon in Canada now, and Philippe is probably supervising some life or death operation.

Still, if he is working his answer phone will kick in and it gives me the excuse to check if my device has survived my stupid temper tantrum.

A few rings out and I'm half expecting a voice message. At least the damn thing is still working.

Then Philippe's cheery voice, the real one rather than a recording.

'Debbie – how the devil are you?'

Now there's a million dollar question.

Chapter 10

Anyone who knows the real Debbie will recognise a pattern. When under stress, make an effort with the old appearance. Dressing for confidence, with make-up and high heels. Trust me, it works every time.

After my phone call with Philippe Roux, I feel much calmer and ready to face dinner with Amy. The glam up is just icing on the cake, giving her the message that her mum is a woman to be reckoned with.

Taking a bit of time with the make-up, gives space to review Philippe's advice. There's hardly anything that this virtual stranger doesn't know about my life so far. When I first met him in Toronto, the story of my late husband's betrayal came tumbling out. At that point he thought I was in Canada to visit an old school friend – the same phony story I told Amy.

Monsieur Roux kept in touch when I had to return to England quicker than expected, thanks to Kevin's stupid road accident. The poor thing had only broken an ankle but I couldn't leave him to wallow all on his own, not when he needed help to get around.

It was Philippe who I turned to for advice when Amy found out about her dad's affair and fled to London. As we were talking, everything else came tumbling out. My teenage pregnancy, the result of a passionate affair with an older man, Peter Davis, someone I still call privately 'Mr DJ.'

It was then that he learned the 'real' story about my trip to Canada, to meet up with my adopted son Andy, his parents, and girlfriend Lauren. Crucially, I also confided that Peter, aka, Mr DJ, still knew nothing about my past pregnancy or indeed his son.

'My word Debbie, what a burden to carry around' was a line I remember him saying, and all I could think was 'God yes'. Yet for years, I did that very thing, barely noticing the weight of the past, drifting through life, pretending that giving away my son could be conveniently airbrushed away.

At first Philippe was cautious about straying into the adopted son part of my story, preferring to stick to the 'safer' problem of Amy and the discovery about her dad's affair.

On that he was adamant. Tell her everything and apologise for my failure to include her. Limit the damage and above all keep her remembering the good things about David. In time she'd get over the anger and move on to acceptance, a bit like the process she went through after David's sudden death. The old mantra that time will heal.

As for that other bombshell, the existence of my adopted son and Amy's half-brother, when Philippe did eventually open up, he suggested that out of the options available – continue to keep it a secret forever or tell my daughter the truth – both had huge risks. Go the secrecy route and if Amy ever found out, there would be emotional carnage. Yet open up about the past and risk the very same.

'If it were me, I'd take the second of the difficult roads. On this though, you are out on your own Debbie. Tough but true.'

Afterwards, when I talked everything through again with my partner Kevin, he had a more definite take on the matter.

'You've buried this for long enough. The time is right to tell Amy – she will prefer that to finding out in some other way and now you're in touch with your son that could well happen. Think about it.'

Of course Andy and his adopted parents have promised faithfully to keep everything between ourselves, if that is my wish. I trust them on that. Still, one revelation can lead to another whether intentional or not and I've just learned that very lesson the hard way.

As for Mr DJ, well here's the other big dilemma. Opening up about my secret past will surely also mean telling him everything which will come as a terrible shock. Then admitting to my adopted son that yes, I really do know who his real father is. As things now stand, Andy is under the illusion that I've got no idea, hence the missing father bit on his birth certificate.

I wonder if life could possibly get any more complicated. Yet the reality of life is exactly that. Complexity, negotiation, resolution. Always has been and will continue to be so.

'Mum, you ready now?' Amy's voice cuts in, silencing my inner debating circle.

A last slick of lipstick, the plum one I've always worn, and the answer is 'yes'.

In far more ways than one.

Chapter 11

'Wow mum, you make me look like a tramp.'

Not that Amy could ever look that way, however casually dressed. Let's face it, devil-may-care youth still triumphs over older glam and there's no way around that.

Still, a compliment is a compliment and I'm not complaining.

'Thanks, I thought I'd make a bit of an effort seeing this is such a smart place.'

'Er, and does that mean I should get changed?' Amy is glancing down at her ripped black jeans and gold trainers.

'Don't be silly, you always look great. Wait until you get to my age and you'll see why slapstick is a girl's best friend.'

We opt to head over to the bar first, both of us keen to try the cocktail Happy Hour. I order my favourite Marguerita while Amy opts for an Aperol Spritz, something she's been introduced to by 'Mr Trust Fund', Ashley.

Now the drinks are in hand, both of us are wary of being first to cut to the chase. In the end it is me who gets things going, casting aside the university situation for now.

'What else would you like to know about your dad and Jemma then?'

'Well then mum, how about all the bits you actually know?' Already she's back on the attack, lower lip jutting out to signal disapproval.

'For a start, Jemma told me that they also used to meet at a hotel in Falmouth, that big one near Gylly beach.'

Amy looks up from examining her drink, a puzzled expression on her face.

'Eh? I thought you said he had a flat in St Agnes?'

'Yes, that too. I can only think that he was borrowing the flat from someone, maybe sub-letting it, and he didn't have access to it during weekdays.'

Amy is stirring her drink, probably trying to get the image of her cheating dad out of her head. Yes, already been there and done that myself, hundreds of times.

'Yuk – it all sounds so sordid. No it is sordid. Sneaking off to hotels when he was supposed to be away working. Dirty bastard.'

That last bit is said a bit too loudly and the elderly man sitting nearby looks over disapprovingly.

'If you're going to use language like that Amy,

keep your voice down.'

'Sorry, but I couldn't help myself. I keep remembering all those times he'd ring home, pretending he was on the road by himself. It makes me feel sick.'

'I know darling but believe me I've been to hell and back thinking the very same. How he'd always tell us he loved us and that he missed not being at home.'

There are a few seconds of silence and an awkward smile from me across to the elderly gent, who has now decided to move onto another table. Unsurprisingly, he doesn't return my non verbal attempt at an apology.

'This flat of his – did you two have any friends in St Agnes?' Again, it's a question I've wracked my brains over and the answer is no. It's a place we visited when we first started to go out, but apart from that there is no other link, friends or otherwise.

'Not as far as I can tell. Me and your dad used to have a favourite pub there when we were younger, we'd go to watch live bands.'

'Yes, I remember dad saying something about seeing some good rock bands there back in the day.'

This was before I came on the scene but it was something David used to bang on about when he dug out his old vinyl records. By the time we went there in the early 1980s, it was a mix of Punk and New Romantic, the Clash and Duran Duran wannabes.

'Maybe that's what drew your dad back there. Music memories, reliving his youth.'

'So Jemma's got no links to St Agnes then?' Amy is still stirring her drink distractedly.

Now I hadn't thought of that but I'm guessing no. If Jemma did have close friends or relatives nearby, then it would be difficult for David to pass off the legend that he was staying there most of the time, alone in a flat. Someone close to Jemma and living locally would know that wasn't true.

'I doubt it Amy. From what I can glean, Jemma was sharing a house with some friends just outside Truro.'

Amy has already finished her drink and is clearly looking for a refill. We've just about got enough time to order another before the Happy Hour finishes.

Funny thing this 'Happy Hour' tradition. Looking around there aren't too many cheery faces, everyone either deep in serious looking conversation or sitting alone examining smartphones, pretending to look nonchalant.

If ever there was a name ill suited now, this would be it.

'Another of those Aperols then?'

Amy nods and I can see that something is still preoccupying her.

'Tell you what mum, why don't we just get Jemma over here tonight? See if she can meet us –

and join up all the missing dots while she's at it.'

Lord, she has to be joking but her face is telling me that she isn't.

'I'm not sure I think...'

The words have barely left my mouth when Amy grabs her phone.

'No mum, we really need to get her over here. No more games – I'm dialling her right now.'

Holy shit.

Chapter 12

'Hi it's Amy here. Amy McKay. When you pick up this message can you give me a call?'

Thank God her call to Jemma has gone into voicemail, a chance to scupper this madcap idea of hers.

'Listen, trying to get Jemma to come here at short notice is stupid. I doubt whether she'll be up for it anyway.'

Amy rolls her eyes.

'We'll soon see won't we? Here. Let me get those drinks before we miss the Happy Hour slot.'

Before I can say anything else, she's stomping her way over to the bar, gesticulating to the waiter. It's actually just gone past Happy Hour but Amy still manages to pull off a second round of cheap cocktails.

Once back, she insists on backing up the voice message to Jemma with a text.

'She'll know it's important if she gets both.'

In my head I reply with a sarcastic 'yeah of course if you say so Amy' but wisely stay silent. I'm confident that Jemma won't set off at Amy's beck and call, especially when she finds out that I'm here too.

Neither of us have eaten much today and my stomach is starting to growl.

'Look, let's head over to dinner and we can carry on our chat there.'

Though hungry, Amy wants to wait for to see if Jemma rings back.

'Can't we just finish our drinks first mum and see if she does want to meet us? She could join us for dinner.'

Ha, bloody ha. What a lovely meal that would turn out to be.

Still, I relent and agree to give it another half hour at the most. My chance to address the university question.

'Now this plan you and Ashley have hatched to go travelling – I still think you should wait until you've both finished your courses.'

Another roll of the eyes and jutting of the mouth.

'Mum, I've told you already. It's happening, end of. We're not kids and can do as we like, just as you did. Remember?'

Oh Amy I remember all right and soon you'll know why.

'All I'm asking is that you press the pause button, keep the plans for when you finish your degrees rather than stopping and starting... that's if you do ever go back.'

'Ah – so that's it? You think we won't finish university, we'll just hang out as hippies in Goa? This isn't the seventies you know. People leave and go back to education all the time.'

We both flinch as Amy's phone pings with an incoming text. And yes, it is from Jemma.

Amy reads out the words.

'Call me back in five on this number.'

'I'm doing it mum, ringing her back - and going travelling. So get used to it, OK?'

Right now I feel like slapping her across the face for her rudeness. How dare she talk to me like this? My look says it all.

'Do what you like then but don't say that I didn't warn you.' My words are spat out, louder than I intended. For once Amy looks taken aback.

I need to get some fresh air to clear my head, before there's a repeat of our earlier row.

'You talk to Jemma if you must but don't count me in.'

'But mum if she comes over tonight, I want you there. It's important we both see her this time.'

'No Amy, I'm butting out. I'll order dinner in my room and you can do damn well what you like. As you say you are all grown up now.'

With that I leave, walking tall on my high heels. Head in the air and crumbling inside.

'Mum you can't just go pissing off...'

Oh yes I can Amy.

Just you watch me.

Chapter 13

Tempting as it is, I'm not going to call Kevin. He's the one who put the phone down earlier and my mood certainly hasn't improved since then.

I've bought along some of the letters from Mr DJ and while waiting for room service to deliver a ham omelette and fries, I've been re-reading them. It's been a good few weeks since I posted off my last letter, the one where I revealed my true age when we first met in 1975. Back then, Mr DJ was a minor celebrity disc jockey, already in his mid thirties but pretending to be just 25 years old. Me, only a few weeks away from my 16th birthday, making out that I was the grand old age of 19 and working in the fashion trade. What on earth were we playing at?

Why did I try to reconnect with him forty years later? Was it really prompted by all those stories about 1970s celebrity DJs, the Jimmy Savile case giving rise to accusations of child sexual abuse and exploitation?

Except not once did I ever believe I was abused. It would be easy for me to take that view and doubtless some therapists would say that I'm in denial. Yet I maintain the belief that I went into the relationship knowing what I was doing and more importantly, wanting it to happen.

Of course, I hadn't planned for the pregnancy and had even managed to get a prescription for contraceptive pills, not that easy in those days. Looking back, it was probably a stomach upset that led to the pill not working and next thing there I was, alone and pregnant. By then Mr DJ had gone off to live in Manchester, unaware that I had 'a bun in the oven' to use the phrase of the time.

My decision to relocate to Cornwall on the pretext of wanting to take a year out between 'O' and 'A' Level exams, is probably why I'm so concerned about Amy wanting to opt out of university to go travelling. A few years down the line, after working in a hotel and giving up my baby for adoption, I did go back to night school and take a couple of 'A' levels. Afterwards I managed to get a place on the local newspaper as a trainee reporter, so didn't go on to university. It's something I still regret even though I've managed to have a good career despite the lack of a degree.

As for Mr DJ, he ended up as a music mogul, well heeled and living in a luxury mansion with another fabulous home in Tenerife. He's not been so lucky in his personal life – he has already gone through two divorces – but has an older daughter and two younger twin boys whom he adores.

When we first began our old fashioned letter correspondence over a year ago, (at the time it seemed an appropriately retro way to do things), I'd gone through heartache with the early death of my husband David. Otherwise, I thought I'd done pretty well on the personal relationships front. Happy marriage of 25 years, lovely daughter - that's until I found out that my relationship with David wasn't all that it was cracked up to be.

Then came the out-of-the-blue approach from my adopted son, Andy, now in his early 40s and living in Canada. Truth be told, Andy was the real reason I contacted Mr DJ, with all that other stuff in the news headlines being mere background noise. The two things just happened to collide, with Andy getting in touch around the same time of the big public debates about social and sexual mores in the 1970s. Yes, coincidences really do occur but as my nan used to say, 'things happen for a reason.' Queen of the cliché was my nan, but on this occasion her overly used expression has a point.

'Hey mum – can I come in? I've just got off the phone to Jemma.'

Amy's voice cuts in violently, my mind wrenched from its memories back into the present.

I quickly gather up Mr DJ's letters, shoving them into a drawer, before opening the door.

Amy doesn't look disturbed, quite the opposite. She's actually smiling and clutching a bottle of wine.

'I've bought this as a peace offering.'

I don't say anything but move across to let her in. Why the smiley face? Surely it can't have been pleasant talking to Jemma, Minx Extraordinaire?

'Don't worry she's not coming over here tonight' Amy announces as soon as she's through the door. 'You were right about that.'

I remain silent, waiting for her to continue.

Amy plonks herself down on the bed, still holding the bottle of wine.

'By the way mummy dear, this cost me a shed load from the bar' she adds, perusing the label.

'There are only a couple of disposable glasses in here' I reply, glancing over to check that I've properly closed the drawer where I've stashed Mr DJ's letters. It's still slightly ajar, so I move across to lean against it.

'I'll ring reception and get some sent up' she says, simultaneously dialling the phone. Already I can see that Amy has got more confident about using hotels and that's likely to be down to Ashley as well. We've never been big hotel users, mainly opting for self-catering and when David was alive he always wanted to avoid hotels.

'I get enough of those with work' he'd say. Now I'd add the line 'and screwing the girlfriend.'

'Want the low down on my chat with Jemma then?' Amy asks as we wait for the glasses to be sent up. My stomach is rumbling now, so I'm hoping the room service food arrives soon.

'I'm guessing that I'm going to hear about it whether I want to or not.'

Amy ignores my jibe, and starts to root in her

handbag for a cork screw.

'We need to let this wine breathe a bit. Thing is, if she hadn't been shagging my dad, I think I'd quite like Jemma.'

I wince at the word 'shagging' which somehow seems cruder than 'screwing'. Or maybe it's just because Amy is using the term.

The cork comes out easily, making a slight popping noise and Amy sniffs the open bottle, wrinkling her nose.

'This had better taste nicer than it smells. Anyway, Jemma was fine about us meeting up, whether you are there or not. She even asked how you were...'

A rap on the door means the arrival of room service and the drinks glasses we asked for. Clearly the hotel has mastered the art of joined up service.

'Are you having anything to eat?' I ask Amy, examining my small omelette and fries. There isn't enough for sharing and she's veggie anyway.

'No, you go ahead and dig in – I've lost my appetite.'

Funnily enough, I'm not surprised that Jemma asked about me. I'm sure she's hoping that there won't be any fall out at her workplace following her dalliance with my late husband and her former boss. 'Dalliance' - now there's an elegant word and much more refined than shagging.

Amy hands me a glass of wine, a French red, and

it tastes delicious. Philippe Roux would certainly approve, that's a given.

'Anyway, me and Jemma didn't talk for long. She's off out this evening with some friends, probably including Carl.....'

'Here at least have a few of these fries' I reply trying to ignore the reference to Carl Martin my magazine boss. Maybe that's Jemma's thing, hitting the sack with her male bosses. I've always taken the view that when it comes to work, promotion is usually based on raw talent.

Well I say 'usually'. In Jemma's case I'm not so sure.

'Nah – I'll stick to this for now, it's a good one isn't it?'

I nod, between mouthfuls of omelette which is no more than passable.

'Jemma is coming over here tomorrow evening after she's finished work.' Amy glances across to gauge my reaction.

Shit. Tomorrow is the day that I need to tell Amy about her adopted half brother. The murky subject of David and Jemma was supposed to be all done and dusted this evening.

'I'd prefer if we could leave off meeting Jemma at least for a few days. I want to talk to you about something else tomorrow.'

'If you think we're going back to the university thing...'

'It's not about university...it's about why I've chosen this hotel.'

Amy is looking quizzical, trying to read between the lines.

'You're not ill or anything..?'

'Of course not, I'm fit as a fiddle. But I want to share something really important tomorrow.'

'Well just do it now – why does it have to wait?'

'Because today is all about the situation with your dad and I didn't want to mix the two things up.'

'Mum, for fuck's sake just tell me. Is this another bombshell I'm going to hear about?'

You could say that Amy.

'Look just put Jemma off for a couple of days. Please.' I'm trying not to sound desperate but failing miserably. Whatever, Amy finally gets the message.

'All right then but I'm not going to drag it out. This thing tomorrow had better be worth it.'

Oh it will be. No question about that.

I glance down at the rubbery and now cold omelette languishing on my plate. Mixed with the wine, I have a sudden urge to throw up.

'You all right mum...?'

Unable to wait long enough to answer, I hurl myself towards the bathroom. Suddenly the expression 'as sick as a dog' makes some kind of sense.

Rinsing my mouth out afterwards, my mind flashes back to the last time I was here all those years ago.

Then it was morning sickness. Now it is simply fear.

Fear of the beast I'm about to unleash.

Chapter 14

After my undignified regurgitating of the rubbery omelette mixed with a well chosen high end wine, it's the perfect excuse to get an early night.

We'll just have to park the David and Jemma situation for now, hoping that some of our unanswered questions are met when we next see the Minx. Like Amy, I have confused feelings about her. She's a victim herself of sorts, a young woman insisting that she was led to believe that David was a free man.

Then again, she certainly didn't seem to ask too many questions. Perhaps she didn't think she needed to, being a trusting soul. Enough women – and men – have fallen for that one over the years.

Still, he was her boss and that alone should have been enough to stop Jemma in her tracks. Yikes, but let's not forget David's role in all of this. Older, supposedly wiser, knowing he was pursuing a younger work colleague.

That's much harder to forgive isn't it? Yet forgive we must because if we don't, all of our previous life together will be destroyed by hatred.

Why am I even still thinking about this now? My

priority ought to be tomorrow's news, telling Amy that she has a half brother and revealing the story of how he came to be adopted.

Back then to tomorrow's plan...if you can really call it that.

First, I'll suggest a walk around the hotel gardens and start by telling her about my relationship with Mr DJ and teenage pregnancy.

I will describe how this place used to be known as a 'mother and baby' home, a sort of half-way house for young women who were expected to give their babies up for adoption.

Of course, I have no way of knowing how Amy will take this news. I can only pray that she will come to understand and that one day she might get to meet her half-brother Andy.

Then there is the question of Mr DJ. True to my promise to tell Amy all, I can't stick to the pretence that I don't know who Andy's real dad is.

Right now I feel like an explorer about to embark on an expedition, with no idea what the outcome will be. Of course for an adventurer it can mean life or death. In my case the stakes aren't that high, thank the Lord, but the fall out could still be catastrophic.

At the end of the day, I've got to hope that everything will work out. Telling the truth after all these years has to be better than the fiction I've been living for decades of my life.

Funny that Andy sent me an email earlier, asking how I was and suggesting a phone chat over the coming weekend. His tone was chirpy and he was about to set off for a romantic few days break with his fiancée Lauren.

'Hiya Debbie,

Hope all is good and this is just to let you know that I'm off to Boston for a mini vacation with my lovely Lauren. We're both in need of a work break and Boston is one of our favourite cities. Can't wait! It would be great to catch up next weekend once we're back and I can tell you all about it. Speak soon and take care. Mom and dad send their good wishes too. Andy. xxx'

Yet again, no fond wishes from 'the lovely' Lauren which is a strange omission, but one that I'm starting to get used to.

Well then, how am I feeling at this late hour? Bizarrely, quite serene, a classic case of a calm before the storm.

As I turn off the light, desperate to get some sleep, there is the distant hoot of a night owl.

Suddenly I'm back in the spring of 1976, counting the rows of roses on the faded wall paper of my room at St Brigid's.

One rose, two rose, three rose...

Rows of once vivid red roses, parading up and down before my eyes.

And the owl, persistent and seemingly getting louder. A good or bad sign of what is to come?

Chapter 15

The hypnotic sound of the owl must have worked its magic because I've just had the best sleep in days and the sun is shining through a chink in the blackout curtains.

It's only 7am and way too early to wake Amy. Instead I put on the kettle, popping an English Breakfast teabag in the mug and opening the complimentary pack of Cornish clotted cream biscuits.

Kevin will be up by now, getting ready for work. After my decent slumber, I'm feeling more mellow than yesterday and a bit ashamed that I dumped my frustration with Amy on him.

He's clearly pleased to hear from me, relieved that I've finally got around to calling him back.

'Debbie - I was about to ring you. Is everything OK?'

Bless him, thinking of me when it is I who should be grovelling about my bad behaviour.

'Fine Kevin and before you say anything else, I hold up my hand to being a prize bitch yesterday. I'm so sorry for upsetting you...'

'Forget it, you were in shock over Amy's news. I should have been more sympathetic rather than slamming down the phone.'

There is a brief silence, each of us unsure how to go on. In the end, Kevin takes the plunge.

'Talking of Amy, how's it all going with you two?'

I give Kevin the low down on my row with Amy, her insistence on contacting mistress Jemma, and then being forced to tell her that I've got even more revelations to unveil today.

'Can you believe that Amy actually wanted Jemma to meet us here today of all days?' Kevin doesn't reply, but gives out a low sympathetic whistle.

He listens as I go through today's plans, as much for my own sake as his. Of course he's heard it before but is polite enough to let me run it past him again.

'Hell I don't envy you this one sweetheart but try to be strong. I'll be thinking about you both and call me as soon as you can.'

'Kevin you know I love you loads, even though I can be a moody cow sometimes' I reply, wishing that he was in the room so that I could give him a big hug. Or best of all, to receive one back.

'Too true but I still love you anyway. Now go and tell that daughter of yours what she really needs to know. '

I take my time getting dressed, choosing a grey shift dress to reflect my sombre mood. I've looked yet again at Mr DJ's letters and will show them to Amy at some point. There's also the booth photograph of me as a teenager with my best friend Charlie and I've tucked that inside my hand bag for safe keeping.

After David died, I was advised by a friend to take a course in Iyengar Yoga to help cope with the stress and I've used the breathing exercises on numerous occasions when calm is needed.

Four deep breaths. Hold to the count of seven and then exhale slowly. Repeat the same six times and then start over again. Odd as it seems, it really does work and already I can feel my body and mind relaxing.

The effect doesn't last for long though, my serenity punctured by the piercing shrill of a fire alarm. Damn it, probably just an exercise and already I can hear footsteps in the corridor.

It will have woken Amy, so I hover outside her door expecting her to appear any minute, all tousle haired and grumpy. When there's no sign, I bang on the door yelling over the painfully loud alarm.

'Could everyone move towards reception please?' A concerned young man is trying to get people to head out of the corridor but I'm not moving without Amy.

'My daughter is still in there. She must have slept through the alarm.'

The young man looks irritated and bangs loudly on the door.

'Can you come out please. This isn't an exercise, there's a real fire. ' He pauses, listening for an sound inside Amy's room.

'Amy for goodness sake, get a move on.' I'm shouting now, while covering my ears which are starting to hurt.

'I'll have to use the master room card I'm afraid' the young man says, reaching into his pocket. He swipes the door and we both enter the room.

Not a sign of Amy. No indication that she's even slept in the bed.

I do a quick scan around the room but there is no bag, no toiletries. Nothing.

'Did your daughter change rooms by any chance?' the young man asks, while I stand there slack jawed and stunned.

'Not that I know of' I finally reply, aware that he really wants us out of this part of the building and fast.

'Come on we have to go' he insists and it's only when I get to reception that I realise just how many people are staying at this hotel. There is a sea of bemused faces, some still in nightwear and others who have obviously just got out of the shower.

It's only then that I realise that I don't have my phone with me - and still no sighting Amy.

Chapter 16

Desperately scouring the hotel crowd for any sign of my daughter, I'm struck by range of ages and types staying here. Then again, it's difficult to know how many of them are staff members living or sleeping on the premises.

We're all standing outside the main reception area and despite the morning sun, it's pretty damned cold. A young woman, I'm guessing around Amy's age, is shivering in a flimsy dressing gown while frantically texting phone messages and taking photos. Watching her makes me even more anxious that I've left my mobile along with everything else, including handbag, inside the room.

The same hotel worker who ushered me down here, is trying to reassure everyone that the fire brigade is on its way.

Where the hell is Amy? She seemed fine last night, as far as I could tell, so why would she not even bother to sleep in her room?

'Excuse me, would you mind if I make a quick call from your phone? Only I can't find my daughter.' Normally I wouldn't dream of asking a stranger such a favour but needs must.

The young woman looks up, eyeing me for trustworthiness.

'Er - I suppose so. Have you told the staff she's missing?'

'Yes, they know. She might have just gone for a walk but I've left my phone in the room. I'll pay you for the call.'

'Nah - no need for that. I've got loads of free call time on there.' She hands me the phone which has a garish gold glittery cover on it.

Amy's number immediately goes into answer phone.

'Hi Amy, I'm downstairs in reception. Where are you? There's been a fire...'

Before I can finish the sentence, I catch sight of Amy and Ashley of all people, heading up the main driveway with seemingly not a care in the world. What the hell is Ashley doing here?

'Here, thanks - I've just spotted her.' I thrust the phone back into the girl's hand and take off in the direction of Amy and that damned boyfriend.

'Hey, what's happening mum? Why are all these people milling about?' Amy is clearly oblivious to anything that has gone on, while Ashley just looks half asleep.

'There's been a fire alarm and you obviously didn't stay in your room last night. I've been worried sick.'

Ashley is blushing and looking awkward, while Amy is staring at me as if I've lost the plot.

'I didn't want to disturb you last night. Ashley turned up unannounced and we decided to book into another room, that's all. Then we fancied a walk in the grounds and arrive back to all this...' She's talking quickly, a sure sign that she's feeling guilty.

'Sorry Debbie. I didn't mean to worry you. I was missing Amy and thought I'd surprise her with a visit. You don't mind do you?' Ashley's moving from foot to foot, still red faced and apologetic.

Like hell I mind. This is an important day for us both, though to be fair to Ashley he has no idea why.

'Hello everyone. We've been told that it's now safe to go back to your rooms. Sorry for the inconvenience but smoke from the kitchen triggered the alarm. Thank you for your patience.' The young staff member looks almost disappointed that the episode is all over and that he'll have to go back to more mundane tasks.

Everyone rushes forward, leaving the three of us standing alone.

'Can I have a quick word with you on my own Amy?'

Ashley takes the hint and heads inside, telling Amy that he'll go back to their room. She gives him a quick peck on the cheek, adding pointedly that she 'won't be long'.

'Shall we get back inside mum? It's cold out here.' It's not so much a question, more of an order and I follow her back into reception desperately trying to think of some way to get rid of Ashley for the rest of today.

Best to cut to the chase, rather than tinkering around at the edges.

'Amy, I know Ashley meant well coming here but I really need us to be on our own today.'

'Yeah, so you said last night but I can't just send him packing now. He's booked the room for two nights and anyway, I want him here.'

Think hard and quickly Debbie. This is way too significant a conversation to involve Ashley.

'I'm only talking about today sweetheart. Do you think Ashley could head over to our house and come back tomorrow?' There's a genuine sense of urgency in my voice which Amy can't fail to notice.

'Hmm – well I suppose so. He gets on with Kevin so they could have a boy's night in watching sport. I'm warning you that this had better be something like really up there.' She's emphasised the 'really' and is looking at me menacingly.

'Trust me, it is. Look, you go and have breakfast with Ashley and I'll meet you outside in an hour.' I give her a reassuring touch on the arm which she doesn't respond to.

Just enough time then for me to head back to my

room and reply to Andy's jaunty email anticipating our 'catch up' over the weekend.

And depending how things develop today, what a mother and son call that could turn out to be.

Chapter 17

In the end I don't have to wait long. Amy calls back to say that they've decided to skip breakfast and Ashley's checking out until tomorrow evening.

'So we can get started on this second chat of yours as soon as you like.'

'See you at the main entrance in five minutes then' I reply, relieved not to have to hang about much longer.

It's already started to warm up outside with the promise of fine weather. It would be lovely to be here simply for a leisurely stay, to enjoy the grounds and facilities, with the option of which facial package to choose being the biggest decision of the day.

Amy looks preoccupied, sensing that something important is afoot.

'Let's stroll for a bit' I suggest, wanting to get further into the grounds, away from the few people taking their before or post breakfast walk.

Nothing is said for a few moments as we head off at a steady pace. The grass is slightly damp and squishy and there's a floral scent which I recognise from somewhere.

'We should bag that bench over there' I suggest, instinctively wanting to start the conversation sitting down. When we get to it, there is a small metal plaque dedicated to Rosemary Grayson 'who loved this place'. Whenever I see these bench memorials, I'm left wondering about the person behind the name. Who are they and what is their story?

'Right then, shoot – get this over with' Amy says as soon as we've taken possession of the seat. She's not making eye contact but staring down at the ground, feet tightly crossed.

A deep breath and then that leap into the unknown.

'You know you asked why I chose this hotel?'

Amy looks up, her eyes now firmly fixed on mine.

'Well - it's because I first stayed here as a teenager way back in 1976.'

She doesn't respond, waiting for me to continue.

'It used to be called a Mother and Baby home back then.'

Her expression stays the same, apart from a slight flicker of the eyes.

'You worked here you mean?' she asks, her eyes widening.

'No, not working. I mean I was here as a

pregnant 16 year old'. There I've said it.

She turns to face me full on, her expression a mixture of shock and confusion.

'What – you said you were pregnant?'

I nod, trying to keep things together.

'Yes and I gave birth to a baby boy who I called Edward. He was then handed over for adoption.'

Amy is trying to take the news in, her arms crossed in a defensive posture.

'You mean like you just gave your baby away?'

I flinch at the 'just' word.

'I finished school and as soon as I found out I was pregnant I set off to Cornwall, telling your nan and grandad that I was going away to work.'

There's a few minutes silence as Amy takes this in.

'So you kept it all to yourself, not even telling your own family?' She sounds incredulous, as well she should.

'Yes and it stayed that way for a long time. Even your dad didn't know.'

Amy jumps up at the mention of her dad and has now turned to face me head on.

'Eh? You didn't tell your own husband?'

I've rehearsed this scene over and over but nothing can prepare you for the real thing.

Absolutely nothing.

I promised myself that I wouldn't cry but here I am, tears cascading down my face. Then the unexpected feel of Amy's arms across my shoulders, her voice soothing and given what she's just heard, surprisingly cool and collected.

'Look...don't get upset mum, just tell me everything from the beginning.'

I nod, reaching down to retrieve a tissue from my hand bag. As I do so, I spot the image of my teenage self staring back from a decades old booth photograph.

A year after it was taken, I was at this very spot and now over forty years on, I'm back here again. My life lurching from rewind to fast forward at a dizzying speed.

Chapter 18

Telling her the first bit was easier as I'd rehearsed it so well. Falling in love with Peter Davis, the man I still call Mr DJ. Him disappearing to Manchester, me finding out I was pregnant just a few months after my 16th birthday and getting my O level exam results.

Amy hasn't said much so far but I know the killer questions will soon be coming thick and fast.

Then the first one.

'Did you ever find out what happened to baby Edward?'

A small pause before the next momentous piece of the tale.

'Not for a long time. Then he got in touch with me almost a year ago.'

Amy's face stays poker straight despite my news.

'So, he made the first approach then?' she's staring into the middle distance now, still no sign of how she is really feeling.

'Yes, we exchanged letters and photos and then we spoke over the phone.'

Out of the corner of my eye, I can see Amy's lower lip quiver, the only small sign of emotion.

'Darling I know this must be upsetting and confusing for you...'

She pushes my hand away, her posture stiffening.

'What does he look like?'

Prepared for this moment, I delve into my bag for a photo. It was taken on my trip to London where we first met. He's smiling broadly, looking relaxed and effortlessly handsome.

Amy stares hard at the picture for several minutes, drinking in the image of the person who is her half brother.

'Where was this taken?'

'It was when I went to meet him for the first time in London – do you remember when I travelled down there with Kevin? I said it was for work but...'

She's still staring hard at the photo.

'Tell me about him.'

I go over the details of Andy's life, explaining the name change, the family move to Canada when he was a young boy, his career as a doctor and psychologist girlfriend Lauren. All the time Amy is looking at the photograph but still listening intently.

'Ah – so that explains the trip to Canada then' she cuts in, finally looking back in my direction.

I nod, acutely conscious of the intricate web of lies I've been spinning.

'I thought it was odd when you came back with no photos of that friend Charlie you were supposed to be visiting. Ashley was suspicious too.'

'I'm sorry that I lied to you about the trip Amy but I wanted to meet Andy again in his home place, to meet his family, before deciding what to do next.'

Amy sniffs, her arms crossed over again in defensive mode.

'Well I've got used to the lies. First dad and then this. Anyway...'

We're interrupted by two hotel workers walking past carrying what looks like a pile of table cloths and napkins, probably heading over to the wedding marquee. They nod as they head across muttering something about 'a lovely day.'

Amy ignores them while I return a smile.

'What were you about to say?' I ask watching the hotel workers saunter into the distance.

'Just to put you in the picture, I read some of those letters from Peter – the old boyfriend you mentioned.' She looks back across to suss out my reaction.

I've heard people describe being 'poleaxed' by news and now I understand what they mean. For once I'm speechless, sitting bolt upright and open mouthed.

'I was in your bedroom looking to borrow a pair of earrings – those silver hoop ones I like. One of them slipped behind the dresser and I took out the top drawer to get to it. That's when I found them.'

It's my turn to remain silent while my mind whirrs. How many of them has she read? I know she hasn't read the last two, the ones where I spoke about David's affair and confessed to Mr DJ about my real age when we got together. I know because I'm still carrying those letters around with me, buried at the bottom of my bag.

The rest though?

'So you know then that I'm back in touch with Peter – I was going to come on to that'. I'm trying not to sound angry about her intrusion but I'm boiling inside. Those were private letters damn it. How dare she?

'If you didn't want me to find them you should have been more careful. Anyway, yes I now get the significance of this Peter or Mr DJ guy. I just thought you were looking up an old boyfriend, too embarrassed to tell me.'

I don't reply, reinforcing my disapproval and then the next truly killer question.

'And I guess you haven't told this Peter guy that he has an adopted son?'

'No Amy I haven't.' I'm welling up again, a mix of outrage and utter shock.

'And Andy? Have you said anything to him?'

One look at my face tells Amy everything she needs to know.

The two hotel workers pass us again but this time there is no cheery greeting.

Our body language says it all – an unequivocal 'do not disturb' sign.

Chapter 19

Turns out that Amy had only seen a couple of the letters – she'd have read more if it hadn't been for Kevin and me interrupting after we arrived home earlier than expected.

It was enough though to discover my past relationship with Mr DJ and to read all about my 'proudest achievements', marriage to David and Amy herself.

'I was so touched by what you said about dad and me' Amy adds, by way of a half apology for intruding into my private mail.

I'm still too stunned to reply and inwardly seething that she has read something of mine in such a cavalier way.

'So where do we all go from here?' she then demands. Indeed. Where the hell do we go?

'I think we should get back home Amy, I've had enough of this place'. Yes it was my idea to come back here, to the spot where Andy was born, but now I just want to be in my own space and bed. Above all I want to be home with Kevin, to have one of his reassuring hugs.

'OK then mum, I can see why.' It's clear that Amy wants out of here too and who could blame her, given what she's just learned?

'Just one more question though before we go. Weren't you completely, like, devastated when they took away your baby?'

I have to be truthful here, however unpalatable.

'No, horrible as it sounds I wasn't. Just relieved to get back to my everyday life, pretend it didn't happen and that's exactly what I did.'

As I say the words, I'm forcing back the tears, while Amy puts her arm through mine. The look on her face a mix of pity and incredulity. Of course I don't expect her to understand, why should she?

We don't say much on the journey home, too engrossed in our own thoughts. Ashley is surprised to see us back so early but senses that it isn't the time to ask too many questions.

While he heads off to make some coffee, Amy lets me know that she has already told him about finding the Mr DJ letters and they'd even Googled his name to get more details.

'In a funny sort of way, I guess this Peter guy and me are also related' she says, looking over to see what effect her words are having.

I don't rise to the bait as it will just make things worse. Besides she does have a point, in her 'funny sort of way'.

'Listen mum, Andrew has to know that you've

told me all about his adoption and his family.'

I nod slowly to indicate that's a given. Of course he must.

'Then we need to tell everything to nan and aunty Carol.'

Again, agreed. Now that things are out in the open, my mum and sister must be told.

It's as if Amy is reeling off a routine checklist of things to be done, like you would a set of household chores. Except with this little list, each comes with an added difficulty, more complexity and potential for hurt.

'And at some point mum... Andrew should know who his real dad is.' She puts emphasis on the real to hammer the point home.

Now that's the much trickier bit. Mr DJ would have to be told first, to prepare him for a likely approach from a son he had no idea even existed. This would require a one-to-one meeting, as it is not something that can be revealed in a letter. Heaven only knows how he will take the news, let alone his own children.

'I don't want to deal with the Peter situation just now Amy. I'm sorry but that one will just have to wait. We've got enough on our plates already.'

Amy doesn't have time to reply before Ashley walks back in, balancing a tray of steaming coffee mugs.

'Er... should I make myself scarce?' he asks,

trying to appear helpful but looking plain awkward.

'Mum we've got to let Ashley in on this – I'm not keeping secrets from him as well.' Amy has gone back to a defensive body mode, arms crossed tightly. Her voice giving out the message that it's an order rather than a polite request.

'All right but please let's all keep things between ourselves for now.' I'm aware of the irony of sharing a secret but asking for them to sit on it for the time being.

A curt nod from Amy shows a reluctant agreement, with the clear post script 'for now'.

Grabbing my cup of coffee, I suggest we all move into the kitchen. This little family saga will take some time reveal to Ashley and the comfort of the kitchen seems the best place to start.

'Once upon a time...'

Chapter 20

To be fair to Ashley, he didn't judge or pass comment. His eyes widened when I got to the bit about my teenage pregnancy and the subsequent adoption, but apart from that he just listened, every so often glancing across and Amy, to check that she was OK.

'Wow' was all he could manage at the end. Yes, wow indeed.

'Hell, and I thought my family was complicated' he then added, taking hold of Amy's hand.

'Mum I think you need to tell Andrew today that I know about him. Me and Ashley will go out for a bit and you can ring him on your own.'

She's right of course. Better to start ticking off that hellish checklist sooner rather than later. He answers the phone straight away, surprised that I've called. Shit, with everything else going on I forgot about his trip away with Lauren.

'Oh hi Debbie. We've just landed in Boston. Is everything OK?'

Then I just blurt it out, unable to go through any niceties beforehand.

'Andy – I've told Amy everything.'

I can hear his intake of breath as he takes in the situation.

'Oh my Debbie. Really? How did she take it?'

There's a different note to his voice, a tightening of the throat. Or is that just me imagining things? We're not on Skype so I can't get any clues from his facial expression.

'She took it quite well really...a lot better than I expected.'

What Andy doesn't know is that the news came on the back of the other devastating stuff about her dad. He also remains clueless that Amy now has some information on his birth father.

I go over the details of my chat with Amy, adding that her boyfriend knows as well. He's listening intently, probably wondering if there are any future difficulties in the pipeline.

'Andy, the thing is she wants to meet you as soon as possible. Of course, you can talk to her on the phone first...'

'That would be great Debbie. I'll need to go through everything first with mom and dad and Lauren. Lordy, I'm completely blown away by this news.'

I can tell that he is and suggest that we leave things until he gets back before arranging a Skype talk between him and Amy.

'Give my love to everyone and I hope they are all OK about this' I add tentatively. Of course I'm still aware that they are not yet in the complete picture but hell, this is a first major hurdle out of the way.

....

Overall things have been much better between me and Amy since our 'big talk' the other day. It's less clear what is going through the boyfriend Ashley's mind and I suspect it's something along the lines of what the hell he's got himself into.

On that score, he's less relaxed in my company and occasionally I've caught him eyeing me as if to say 'has she really kept all that to herself since before I was born?' At his age, everyone is an old biddy after the age of 40, let alone a woman who is now in her sixth decade.

Meantime, Amy has stuck rigidly to her guns about our meeting over at St Agnes with mistress Jemma. With the all other stuff now swirling around in her life, I assumed that the Jemma situation would fade into the background. Yet Amy is as keen as ever to tie up those loose ends with her dad's former mistress.

So that's exactly where we are heading now, only the day after of my phone conversation with Andy.

'Mum I can't wait to speak to Andrew myself – I'm dead excited.' She's checking her hair in the car passenger mirror, despite the real effort she's already made for meeting Jemma. For the time being at least, she's using Andy's full name but I think that will change once they've spoken to each other.

'He's excited too and it's all set up for Sunday evening. Oh for goodness sake Amy, stop using that mirror, you look great.'

Amy snaps the mirror back into place, swapping scrutiny of her locks for an examination of her phone. I'm happy for the temporary silence as I try to imagine what reaction Andy is getting from his parents and now fiancée. They'll be pleased and anxious all at once, probably wondering what the future holds for our newly extended family.

Now there's Jemma to face. We're meeting at the pub that David and I used to go to as a much younger couple, newly married and madly in love. I've not set foot in there for over a decade and wonder whether it has changed much over the years.

As if reading my thoughts, Amy comes up for air from perusing her phone.

'What's this place like we're going to then?'

'We took you to lunch once when you were little. It is right down near the beach – Ashley would love it because it's full of surfers.'

'Can't say I remember it' she replies, just as we pass the sign welcoming us to St Agnes. It's a tricky drive down a tight winding lane which leads down to the pub car park and I need my wits about me to spot cars coming the other way, inevitably far too quickly. It's a relief to finally get there, the car still unscathed.

'Oh yes I remember it now' Amy announces as she glances over to the blue washed Driftwood Inn, which looks much smarter than I recall. There are several people sitting outside, despite the cool temperature and then I spot Jemma, scanning the horizon for any sign of us.

'Hey there she is' Amy points across before waving over in mistress Jemma's direction. Anyone would think we were heading for a gossipy get together with not a care in the world.

Instead we've got the trickiest of conversations ahead and then the promise of seeing the very place that David pretended was his single guy flat. Hardly the upbeat experience it might look like to the gaggle of drinkers looking on.

Chapter 21

Leaving Amy and Jemma on their own, I head off to order drinks. Just coffees for now with the prospect of lunch later, that bit all depending on how things pan out.

Jemma is dressed for the seriousness of this occasion and is wearing a navy blue trouser suit and a grey striped shirt. Her hair is scrapped back in a ponytail and she's pared down the make-up. It's as if she is trying to look the polar opposite of a sex siren and more like someone heading off for a job interview.

There's little in the way of small talk, with Amy making sure we get straight down to the nitty gritty, demanding to know the full 'who, what, why, where and when?' of mistress Jemma's relationship with my late husband. To be fair, Jemma takes all this straight on the chin and seems to be answering truthfully. The only time she visibly flinches is when Amy asks about the Falmouth hotel 'assignations'.

'I mean, didn't you ever wonder why dad wanted you to go to a hotel when he already had a place of his own?'

Jemma looks away, clearly thrown by the

question.

'Dave said something about letting a friend use his flat from time to time and that it was, you know, romantic to go to a hotel as a treat.' As she says this her face reddens, and she's gone back to the nervous habit I noticed before – twisting her watch strap to within an inch of its life.

Already I can tell what Amy's thinking, something along the lines of: 'Yuk way too much information.' Immediately those imaginary pictures of Jemma and David making love, if that's what you can really call it, come flooding back. Try as I might to edit them out, they continue to dominate my thoughts with a potent mixture of jealousy, anger and revulsion.

'Well Jemma, I think dad was a bloody full on shit to us all. Me and mum the most - but you too.' Amy's eyes have started to well up and she feigns the need to go and get some fresh air, leaving Jemma and me by ourselves for a few minutes.

'Honestly Debbie, if I could do anything to make this better for you both, I would. Amy's right though – Dave did behave in a terrible way and we're all the worse for it.'

When Amy gets back I can see she's been crying, a sure sign that she's beginning to draw a line under the story of her dad and Jemma. In the circumstances we decide to skip lunch and head straight to the love nest flat, which is only a short walk from the Driftwood Inn.

'I suppose this was your regular drinking place back then?' I ask as we head out, me narrowly avoiding tripping up on a black Labrador lying down by the door. The owner apologises, pulling him out of our way – that's Cornwall for you, dogs and people always vying for the best spots in the pubs.

'Not really, we didn't come here very often. Dave didn't seem to like it much.'

I'm surprised by her answer. Back in the day, this was definitely his favourite place to drink and catch those rock bands when they were performing. Guilt and too many happy memories of our time together here? I suspect so.

'Here it is – number 11' Jemma announces as we approach what looks like a converted granite three storey house. The door shows three bells – flats 11a, b and c.

'Ours was the top one' she announces. 'Ours' – I wince at that small word, implying as it does, cosiness and intimacy.

The curtains in the ground floor flat twitch as we stand staring up at the windows of 11c. Then there's a loud tap on the downstairs window, the face of an elderly woman appearing out from behind the curtains.

'That's Ethel, she's still living here then.' Jemma smiles across at the image in the window. Within seconds, Ethel is outside the door, greeting Jemma as a long lost friend.

'It's you girl – I thought it as much. Changed your hair colour but it suits you.' Her accent is a rich Cornish one, buttery and warm.

She and Jemma hug, each telling the other that they look well. True in Jemma's case but not so with Ethel who is bone thin with deeply lined leathery skin. I'm guessing she must be 90 if she's a day but mentally seems as sharp as a tack.

How to introduce us? We could say, 'hi we're the wife and daughter of that cheating philanderer David' but in the circumstances that would hardly be appropriate. Instead Jemma jumps to the rescue introducing 'my two friends from Truro.'

Ethel insists that we come in for a drink and I can see that Amy is desperate to look inside the building. Ethel's tiny sitting room is what you might expect, cluttered with stacks of nick-knacks and items on virtually every surface. It's spotlessly clean though, with no visible dust.

'I heard what happened to poor David' she says once we've moved around enough stuff to find somewhere for us all to sit. 'Such a lovely man and taken away so young.'

None of us respond, which Ethel reads as a mark of respect and her cue to move the subject on. She insists that we try some of her home made scones – 'the best in Cornwall my dears, trust me on that' – and disappears into the kitchen. Amy jumps straight in with a question to Jemma.

'Any chance of us seeing the upstairs flat?'

She doesn't have time to answer before Ethel appears around the kitchen door, obviously overhearing what has been said. Nothing wrong with her ears then.

'If you want to see your old flat I can do that for you – there's no one living there now, the people who were last in left a few months ago. The landlord has given me the keys so I can let people look around. Not that we've had that much interest mind you.'

I can see from Jemma's face that she's not at all keen. Amy on the other hand, is like a greyhound out of a trap.

'We'd like to see it wouldn't we mum?' she says, her eyes daring me to refuse.

'I hope you don't mind but I'd rather not' Jemma jumps in, adding quickly that it would be 'way too upsetting' for her. All those sad memories.

Ethel pats her on the shoulder and raises a boney hand across to a faded biscuit tin, retrieving the keys.

'You'll need to give it a good turn, the lock's a bit stiff.' She passes over the keys to Amy, her age mottled hand shaking. 'There you are dear, take your time, there's no rush.'

Leaving Jemma with Ethel, we make our way up the stairs, the very ones that David probably climbed hundreds of times. Ethel is right about the lock and it takes several goes to get the door to open. Once inside, the decor couldn't be more different from old Ethel's. The walls are a mix of tasteful neutrals and the furniture modern, what Amy might call 'funky'. There's a sitting room dominated by a large lilac 'L' shaped sofa and a wall mounted flat screen TV. A framed Auguste Rodin print of a dancing woman graces the back wall, just the sort of thing David would have loved.

'Bet dad chose that' Amy says, echoing my thoughts exactly.

There's only the one sitting room, a small kitchen and a sizeable bedroom. Our eyes are immediately drawn to the king size bed with its cream throw and silver metal headboard. We're both thinking the same thing. Was this their bed?

'Well it's a bit disappointing to be honest, quite pokey' Amy says, pulling back the bedroom window blind. 'Nice view though.'

And it is a good one. Countryside to the left and what an estate agent might call 'sea glimpses' to the other side. I'm still trying to clear my mind of Jemma and David in bed, to be all that enamoured by the scenery.

'Isn't it a bit of a let down, sad and sordid?' Amy asks, the question aimed at herself more than me.

I nod, wondering why on earth David sought refuge here from our lovely family home with all its memories and shared stories. There must have been a deep layer of misery or discontent there, none of which I saw or even thought to look for.

We've seen enough though and after politely

downing one of Ethel's admittedly delicious scones, we say our goodbyes. Jemma and Ethel promise to keep in touch. They won't of course.

As for us, we don't make any guarantees to meet with Jemma again. In my view what is done is done, a curtain drawn on that part of my life with a painful lesson learned.

'I still like Jemma you know' Amy says, as we head back to the car. 'I actually still feel sorry for her if that doesn't sound stupid?'

'I certainly don't, I reply, not altogether truthfully. In another world, yes she'd be an agreeable companion, a sociable work colleague. But she's still partly responsible for that horror movie that is playing on a constant loop in my head.

David and Jemma in the throes of passion. Amy and me in blissful ignorance, believing him when he told us we were his 'best girls' and the love of his life. On and on, over and over, those tortuous memories I'll have for the rest of my life.

Chapter 22

It's me, Andy Speaking...

Hi – Dr Andrew Wilson speaking, or plain old Andy to those who know me. I've got some patient rounds to do in the next hour, so I need to concentrate. That won't be easy after the phone call I got a few days ago from Debbie in England.

What a conversation that was, quite a staggering bit of news. Made all the more weird because I'd just got off a plane in Boston, with Lauren and me looking forward to a mini break in our favourite US city.

Lauren had gone off to buy some sunglasses from an airport store, so I was alone when I took the call. Thank God for that, because it was the sort of call you need time to digest, to wrap your head around.

'Andy – I've told Amy everything.'

Yes, she's finally gotten round to telling her daughter about me, my existence and my adoption all those years ago. If I was a betting man, I'd have said the chances of her doing that were pretty slim. My fiancée Lauren has also gone along with this, convinced that Debbie would never risk upsetting her daughter, her mom or her sister.

To be fair, my folks were much less sure, saying that it wouldn't surprise them if further down the line Debbie decided to open up to her family about the past. 'Truth always has a habit of coming to the surface' my dad said and given that he used to be a police officer, he should know.

Still, it was a shock to get that call so quickly and tomorrow I actually get to speak to my half sister Amy. Yes, I've seen the photos and heard all about her from Debbie but this time we'll be connecting for real. She's a good deal younger than me, only 19, so I'm feeling more like an uncle than brother if you get my drift. Truly though, I can't wait to hear her voice and if all goes to plan, we might even get to meet up pretty soon.

Wow.

Right now, I really need to ring the folks and Lauren - I deliberately didn't tell her during our getaway, tempting as it was. No, it was our few days away, and it had to be just about us. Lauren won't be happy that I've kept it from her, but I'm sure she'll understand. Right now isn't ideal but at least it'll give them a chance to digest the news before we all meet up this evening. Me and Lauren usually have dinner with mom and dad on a Saturday and by sheer good fortune we're due over there tonight.

Unusually it is mom who answers the phone

first, surprised that I'm calling from work.

'Hi son – everything all right?'

My mouth feels dry, so I manage a quick clear of the throat before answering.

'Hey mom, I need to make this short but Debbie has phoned with some amazing news. Guess what? She's only gone and told Amy all about us, the adoption, you, me, the lot.'

I can hear her surprised intake of breath as she digests this information.

'My, my – hey Joe, get over here. Listen to this...' As she gives dad the news, her voice is a mixture of excitement and concern.

When dad gets to the phone, they start to talk over each other.

'Hey. One at a time!' I admonish them jokily, wishing I'd grabbed a glass of water before making the call. My throat now feels like coarse sandpaper.

Mum gets in first.

'How did Amy take the news? It must have been a great shock.'

'Seems like she was fine about it according to Debbie' I reply, adding that Amy and me are going to talk on Skype tomorrow evening.

'And how about you son – are you OK with it all?' Good old dad, always alert to my feelings.

'Hey dad – I'm delighted. I get to know a half

sister who I didn't even know existed until recently. Nervous but yeah, dead pleased.'

I tell them that I've got to dash but that we'll talk about it later.

'What about Lauren - what does she think?' mom asks, assuming I've already told her.

'She doesn't know yet mom, I'll grab a glass of water and then call her. See you later.' Before she can answer, another voice cuts in.

'Dr Wilson – can you get down to room 20 as soon as? Your patient is yelling for you and won't take no for an answer.'

Nurse Sheridan looks flustered and the glass of water, along with the call to Lauren, will just have to wait.

In the life if a busy hospital, personal matters take second place however epic. That's what goes with the territory, as every medic will tell you.

Chapter 23

Siblings Talking...

When it finally comes to the Amy and Andy introduction, I keep my bit short and sweet. Amy has spent hours getting prepared, both physically and mentally, for this first talk with her adopted half brother, and yet again looks like she's stepped straight out of the pages of a glossy style magazine.

'It's only a Skype call, he's not going to be scrutinising your clothes or hairstyle' I say, quickly adding that yes, she really does look amazing.

'Well mum I don't want to look like a tramp' she responds, looking across at my – how shall I put it? – more casual attire of jeans and a baggy shirt.

'You never look like a tramp and trust me your appearance won't be at the front of Andy's mind. He'll be much more interested in you, the person.'

Was I ever so obsessed with appearances? Probably, but that is often, (and perversely), at times when I'm feeling least confident. Then the clothes and make-up are a front, a bit like a coat of armour. Come to think of it, that's exactly what Amy is doing, covering up her nerves with a show stopping dollop of glamour. She's my girl all right.

When Andy's image appears on the computer screen he looks nervous and unsure, mirroring what I last saw in London when we met in person for the first time.

Amy and me are sitting alongside each other and after the briefest of ice breakers, with yours truly smiling and pointing from one to the other – 'OK you pair, her Amy you Andy' – I simply leave them to it.

It's tempting to hang around in the background but that feels way too intrusive. No, this is their private meeting and it should remain that way. Amy has promised not to mention anything about his real father and I have to trust her on that.

After half an hour of work distraction in the study aka 'home office', I wend my way to the kitchen where Kevin is busy preparing this evening's meal, a homemade lasagne. The smells are delicious and there is always something quite sexy about a man who is confident about cooking. I try to ignore the war zone of piled up dishes and discarded bowls, knowing that the end product will surely justify the messy means.

'Before you say anything, it'll all be cleared away once the lasagne is in the oven.'

He's getting his defence in early but tonight the issue of 'not clearing up as you go along' remains unsaid.

Instead I perch on one of the kitchen stools,

grabbing an opened bottle of red wine and pouring myself a large glass.

'Smells divine Mr Chef. Do you want a glass of vino while you're at it?'

Kevin nods, stirring a mix of finely chopped carrot, celery and onion and adding an extra dollop of olive oil.

'How's the big talk going on in there?' he asks as I hand him a glass of wine, still trying not to look disapprovingly at the pile of stuff on the sink draining board.

'It's still going which is a pretty good sign I think'. I'm half tempted to head across and lurk outside the sitting room door to gauge the feel of the conversation. How sad is that?

'Amy looks like she's auditioning for a Hollywood film' Kevin quips, pouting his lips and ruffling his hair. 'Talk about over the top.'

'Ah she's just nervous bless her, it's a way of coping. You were young once, remember...?'

I'm standing behind Kevin now, arm around his waist and head resting on his shoulder. He's still stirring his 'holy trinity' vegetable mix but squeezes my hand affectionately, before telling me off for distracting a man while he's at work. Suddenly I feel lucky to have him in my life, my best buddy with definite benefits.

'Yuk – you two should get a room!'

Amy is standing behind us, a vision in cream lace

top and short black leather skirt. Straight away I'm looking for any signs of upset or concern but there are none. Instead she looks relaxed and – dare I say it? – pretty damned happy.

'Mum, Andy is just fantastic, way too gorgeous to be a half brother. What an amazing bloke, I could have talked to him all night.'

I want to ask loads of questions but Kevin gives me a look that says: 'shush, let her tell you in her own time.'

As it is, we don't have to wait long. After the initial gushing, she gives us a rundown of everything they talked about. His adoption, move to Canada, his fiancée, parents and me. I resist the urge to find out what he said about yours truly, it can wait for another time.

'Of course he wanted to know all about my life, Ashley, uni...' I wince at the reference to university, wondering if she's told him about the latest travel plans.

She doesn't say and I know that it's best not to bring the subject up again. Tonight of all nights, we don't need another row.'

'Anyway, here's the thing mum. He's planning to come over here soon with Lauren, so we'll get to meet for real. Isn't that great?'

I'm trying to look enthused but everything is starting to happen a bit quickly. That innocuous little word 'soon' is worrying, especially if razor sharp Lauren is going to be in tow.

'Mum - aren't you pleased?' Amy has picked up on my non verbal signs of concern, as only she can.

'Of course I'm pleased darling. It'll be great.'

'Tell you what Kevin, that lasagne better be done quickly I'm starving.' In typical Amy fashion, she's flicked the conversation straight over to food while my brain has gone into overdrive.

Mr DJ. Peter. Mr DJ. His name is up there in lights inside my head, bright and garish, unable to be ignored.

'Listen madam, good things can't be rushed. You'll just have to wait.' Kevin's words are of course only referring to our impending dinner.

Yet they could just as easily be relevant to our lives right now.

Chapter 24

The morning after the big introduction to her half brother, Amy is still buzzing.

'Hey when me and Ashley go travelling we can include a trip to Canada to meet Andy's parents.'

'Hmm...' I respond distractedly.

'Did you hear what I just said mum? We can...'

'Yes, yes go and visit Andy. I heard what you said first time.'

Yet again, it occurs to me that all of their first names begin with 'A', which is quite a coincidence. In all honesty, I'm trying not to think about her going off to Canada with that boyfriend of hers. Trying not to second guess what could be teased out of her through Lauren's forensic questioning. Overall, just trying not to brood over any of it and concentrate on packing my stuff for a work interview I've got today with an event organiser.

'You seem grouchy this morning mum, I'd have thought you'd be delighted about how well me and Andy got on.' Amy's now standing across from me, arms folded in readiness for a verbal spar.

'Sorry darling but I've got to get going soon and I

need to check that I've got everything for today's meeting. We can talk about it later, OK?'

Seemingly mollified, Amy shrugs and turns to fill the kettle. Giving her a quick peck on the cheek, I set off to check the post before heading out to the car.

Underneath the usual mix of bills and flyers, there is a cream envelope with that unmistakable writing. Mr DJ's latest letter, after a two month gap.

Appointment or not, I can't wait to open it and after a quick manoeuvre off the driveway and pulling into a nearby cul-de-sac, I tear into the envelope, getting that tell tale whiff of Mr DJ's expensive signature aftershave.

'Hello Debbie,

First of all sorry that it has taken me, (once more !), a long time to reply to your last letter. What a letter it was and I must confess that I was shell shocked by the news that you were just 15 when we first met. You certainly looked and seemed a lot older and I never doubted your claim to be 19 and working in the fashion industry.

If I'd known, I would never have got involved and my guess is that is why you disguised your true age. It has occurred to me that technically I've committed a crime and although I had no idea at the time, it makes me feel more than a bit ashamed.

It's good of you to reassure me that it was what you wanted and I can hardly scold you when I was lying about my own age.

Still Debbie, what we did was wrong even though it was all those years ago. It makes me feel grubby and uncomfortable, to tell you the truth. That's all I'll say on the matter for now but it will take me a while to get over this bolt out of the blue news.

Changing an awkward subject, I'm so glad that you met with Jemma and found it helpful. Trust me you will get to live with the hurt and things will get better. I hope by now that you've sorted things out with Amy, explaining to her why you did what you did. She will come around to it, again trust me on that. Hopefully, she'll keep the good memories of her dad alive despite her feelings of betrayal.

Next my own bit of news and it's not good Debbie, so prepare yourself. For a few months now I've been getting a constant pain in my right side, sometimes it's been quite bad. Like most men I know, I'm not great with doctors, so I left it a long time before the pain got the better of me.

Anyway, after loads of tests, I was called in by the doc and he told me that I've got a cancerous tumour on my liver. It's growing quite fast, so they are going to operate on it next week. There aren't any guarantees that they'll get rid of it but there's no option – it is surgery or going to meet my maker a lot more quickly than I expected.

Of course I'm scared shitless and my daughter Lulu has been a fantastic support. I haven't told the twins yet, not the full details anyway. They just think daddy has to go in for a routine operation and their mum thinks the same too. It's just you and Lulu who know the real story.

Then there's the good bit of news – Lulu is four months pregnant, so if I come out of this in one piece I get to be a grandad. Poor Lulu, having to juggle her great news with a worry about me but she seems to be coping well.

I guess all that boozing over the years has finally caught up with me Debbie. Still, I must be hopeful and I want to be around to see that little grandchild of mine grow up. It will mean reining back the booze and cigars then but hey – I've had a great time while it lasted.

Given my news, I would really like to speak with you and perhaps even meet up once I've got the operation out of the way. If all goes well, I'll be recuperating in Tenerife and maybe you could visit me there? I've put my direct phone line at the bottom of this and it would be great to hear your voice after all this time.

I'll leave things there for now and sorry to be the bearer of bad news, given all your own problems. Keep strong and give me a call as soon as you can.

Love,

Peter xxx

Chapter 25

Cancer. Tumour. Cancer. That's all I can think about.

Heaven knows how I got through the meeting with my work client. Yes, of course I made notes and nodded in all the right places. Yes, I've picked up over £20,000 of new business, which will please my boss Carl.

And now I'm driving back home, numb with shock and in no state to ring Carl to tell him about my sales triumph.

Cancer. Tumour. Such ugly words, both individually and collectively – especially when joined together.

Somehow I've managed the drive home and all I can think about is calling Mr DJ. Perhaps I should just stop referring to him as that because it feels so inappropriate and undignified in the circumstances?

First though, I need a stiff drink to steady my nerves and to give boss Carl the good news before the bad. 'Good' that I've secured a decent contract for the magazine. 'Bad' that I've gone down with an awful mythical migraine attack and won't make the office group meeting this afternoon.

In the event, the good stuff has cancelled out the bad, with Carl even promising to take me for a slap up celebratory lunch later this week.

If only he knew the real reason behind my calling in sick, he'd appreciate what a rubbish suggestion this is but I go along with the idea just to get him off the line. Then a large vodka and tonic, purely for 'medicinal purposes' as the saying goes. Straight down the hatch and no messing about.

With shaking hands I dial the phone number at the bottom of the letter and once again I'm back to my awkward 16 year old self, nervous as hell, heart thumping.

It rings out for a long time and I'm about to give up when a voice cuts in. Not Mr DJ's but a female one, sounding as though she has sprinted to answer the phone.

'Hello...Lulu here.'

Ah Lulu. I hope the fact that she's around at her dad's house, doesn't mean bad news.

'Hi is Peter there?'

A slight pause as she tries to make an assessment. Nuisance call? Friend? Or something else?

'He asked me to call him' I add before she has a chance to say anything else.

'Can I tell him who it is?' she asks, sounding wary and still trying to steady her breathing. Of course she's pregnant, so that might explain the breathlessness.

'It's Debbie McKay' I reply, wanting to sound more relaxed than I really am.

'I'll just go and get him Debbie. He's out in the garden so it will take a few minutes.'

Her voice is pleasant, what my mum might have called 'quite posh' even. Like a softly spoken BBC newsreader, easy on the ear but still with an air of authority.

A few minutes seem like an age. I wish I could calm down but that isn't going to happen. Then the voice, the one I haven't heard in over forty years.

'Debbie – my God, is that really you?'

He sounds surprised that I've picked up the phone, which is strange given his clear invitation to call.

'Yes Peter it's really me. I got your letter this morning and had to speak to you as soon as I could. You are all right to talk now I take it?'

'Of course and delighted to hear your voice. You sound exactly how I remember it – no Cornish accent then!' He's trying to lighten the mood, ignoring my reference to the letter. His voice sounds different, with less of a Birmingham accent.

'You sound – er – a bit better spoken than I recall' I reply, adding that no, I haven't taken on a Cornish burr. Doubtless my sister would beg to differ - always telling me that I'm sounding far more 'West Country' these days.

He's listening, still drinking in my voice.

'Ha – I'm no longer much of a Brummie but the odd word sort of just slips out. You can take the boy out of Birmingham but...'

'Dad – do you still want a cup of tea?' Lulu's voice comes in and she's clearly hovering in the background.

'Hang on a sec Debbie – yes I'll have a tea darling. No rush though, whenever you're ready.' I can hear her exiting the room and the soft closing of a door.

'Sorry about that Debbie – that's Lulu as you know. She insists on coming over every day at the moment, not that I mind really.'

As he speaks, I can feel myself calming down. The heart rate is slowing and my mind kicking back into gear.

'Peter, how are you? I was pretty shocked by your news.' I don't want to put off the real reason we are both speaking now, replacing our usual exchange of letters.

'Do you mind if I grab a cigar before we carry on our chat Debbie? I might not be able to drink anymore but I'm not giving up on the baccy yet.'

'Go ahead' I reply, steeling myself up for what is going to be the most awkward of conversations. You'd think I'd be getting used to those tricky talks by now, with the roller coast ride I've been experiencing over the past few months. I'm trying to imagine him, sitting in his palatial pad, box of cigars at his side and open views across the beautiful countryside. This is all in my head, I have no idea of the layout of his home but I've seen pictures of the surrounding area and it looks stunning.

'Right then Debbie. I'm all set. But please let's start with you first. How's that lovely daughter of yours?'

Lots of things have changed over four decades but one thing at least has stayed the same. Peter takes the lead and everyone else follows.

And if that's how he wants it, that's fine by me.

Chapter 26

The 'old' Debbie, as I now refer to myself before the recent momentous changes, was never one for reunions. Over the years I've had invitations to attend get together parties with former school friends but have always turned them down.

I reckon if you haven't kept in touch with people for over forty years, why would you want to do it now? They won't be the same people and neither will you. It would be like talking to complete strangers, desperately trying to find some remnant of an age old connection which was really only a fleeting one in the first place.

No, the old Debbie was all about the present and seeing the past as something that has been and is – crucially – now gone.

But now look at me, not only reunited with my adopted son but his father too. What was once pushed away in the outer reaches of my mind, filed away under 'that was then', is dominating my everyday thoughts.

My telephone conversation with Peter, (yes I have finally ditched the 'Mr DJ' moniker), lasted over an hour but it felt much shorter. After a few minutes we were talking as if we were back in his Birmingham flat, debating the merits of reggae versus ska, soul versus rock music.

Our recent exchange of letters helped here, filling in historical gaps and giving an up-to-date portrait of ourselves. To some extent, we both already knew each other's lives, hopes, dreams and now fears.

It took a while for Peter to properly open up about his health scare, using the distraction technique of my own life events to put things off. We got the awkward subject of the past lies about our ages out of the way pretty quickly. At one point we even managed to laugh about it, though I could tell that he was still troubled by the fact I was so young when we first got together.

Of course the proverbial elephant in the room was our adopted son and it took a lot of willpower for me not to blurt out the news. The switch of conversation back to Peter's health situation turned out to be the saviour here.

'Now Peter that really is enough about me. I want to know how you got on with your doctors and what's going to happen next.'

When he did start to speak about it, his worry was obvious. The tumour was advanced and might mean removing a good chunk of his liver. It would be a tricky operation but if all went well, he would be able to carry on and potentially have a reasonable quality of life.

'Well a life without fine wines Debbie and I'll

have to get rid of my drinks cellar.'

I could hear him puffing hard on his cigar, as if to reinforce his one and only remaining vice.

'Tell you what though. If you come over to visit me here, I can watch you enjoy those wines.'

'And do you really want me to visit you Peter? What will you tell your children?'

Another puff on his cigar and the answer was clear.

'That you're an old friend who has got in touch, the truth in other words. Why do you ask?'

'Ah, so they already know about our exchange of letters?' I'm not sure why, but I assumed that like me, he'd kept our correspondence between ourselves.

'Of course. Why would I keep it from them? I always tell Lulu everything and she knows all about your life and us. That's OK isn't it Debbie?'

'Yes that's fine' I replied, trying to keep the surprise out of my voice.

'And I take it you've also told Amy about contacting me?' he asked, probably picking up the giveaway tone of my voice.

I replied that yes, Amy knew about our correspondence, without going into the how and why.

'So once this little operation is knocked on the head, I'll be setting off to the sun to recover. Why don't you and Amy come over? Bring that man of yours Kevin too if you like.' He's already assuming that it's a given, a trip to Tenerife to see him in a month or so, depending on how quickly he gets over what is far from a 'little' procedure.

'Let's see how it all goes first Peter but it would be lovely to see you at some point.'

We left it at that, trip likely but with nothing confirmed yet. I wished him all the best for his operation in four days time and promised to ring straight afterwards to check on how everything had gone.

'Get in touch with that PA cum daughter of mine first as I'll be in a haze of drugs for a while. A bit like back to the 70s then, eh?' He laughed at the drugs reference but there was a palpable tension there that we both couldn't ignore.

'Take care Peter and I'll be thinking about you.'

End of the conversation, for now at least, and there was no getting away from the fact that if he survived this massive health scare, he'd have to be told about Andy.

His illness has changed everything and whatever the consequences, he can't be kept in the dark any longer.

Neither can our son.

Meantime, I can only pray that Peter will pull through, please God.

Chapter 27

New Year, New Diary...

My expensive pale blue suede diary is open at the start of a new year. It's a Christmas present from my partner Kevin and he joked about the coming year 'hopefully being a much bloody calmer one than the last'. Hand on heart, if this time last year you'd asked me to predict what was in line for the next twelve months, I'd have laughed you out of the room.

Big time.

Yes, without doubt, the past few months have been the most momentous of my life. At one point I feared that whichever way I turned, there would be an immovable barrier to happiness and a harmonious life.

How wrong that was. Despite the worry, anxiety and at times downright fear, life has a habit of sorting itself out. It may not always be in the form of those nice neat solutions that seem to come so easily to other people, but somehow things do work out for the best.

Now as I prepare to pack away last year's diary,

this where I am today and a glimpse of what might lie ahead.

First of all, I no longer have any buried secrets. My adopted son, Andy, now knows all about his birth dad and vice versa. More on that subject later.

My mum and sister also know the truth. They still haven't got over the shock and I doubt if they ever will. At least we are back on speaking terms, something which looked unlikely just a few months ago.

Peter is still recuperating from his operation and it will be a long slow road to full recovery. He had over fifty per cent of his liver removed and lost several stones in weight – not that he needed to in the first place.

Peter's children from both of his marriages are also in the picture, with all of them coming slowly to terms with their new larger 'blended' family.

Meantime Amy is preparing to visit her half-brother in Canada for an extended stay. As planned, she has taken a year out of her degree course but isn't going to travel the world with her now ex boyfriend. Instead she's going to combine a stay with Andy and his adopted family, with a short term placement at Toronto University.

As for Ashley, he was devastated by their break up and decided to console himself by heading off alone for a trip to the Far East. As far as I know, their relationship sort of just fizzled out, probably due to the big changes within our family. Who knows? Perhaps it wasn't meant to be.

I can't say I'm entirely happy with Amy's decision to put her UK studies on hold but at least she'll be spending time with her new extended family and with it, the opportunity to bond properly with her brother.

How has it affected our relationship? Not as badly as I'd feared it might. She's still working through the discovery about her late dad's affair – as I am – but as far as her new half-brother is concerned, she is both delighted and excited. She's still the same feisty, funny and caring daughter that she always has been but now without a regular boyfriend.

So how did we finally arrive at this point? Well here's how it happened, messily at first but getting easier as the weeks passed by.

After my first phone call with Peter, his daughter Lulu kept me up to date with his progress. The operation went well but it was clear that there would a long rocky road back to health. Also, there could be complications, especially if he were to go down with any kind of post operative infection.

As soon as he was considered fit enough to travel, Peter went to his house in Tenerife. It wasn't long before I got a call from Lulu to say that although still physically weak, he was keen for me to visit. I was unsure about taking up his offer to bring Kevin and Amy along with me, but he insisted that I should. Of course, Peter being Peter, got exactly what he wanted and in July we all flew over to meet him in Tenerife.

As soon as we landed I knew that if he was well enough to take the news about our son's existence, then this was the time he should hear it. Here's a quote from my diary, describing the day I finally gave him the news:

'That's it then diary. Today I did what I needed to do – tell Peter the full story about his son. We were alone, the heavily pregnant Lulu having gone off with Amy and Kevin on a trip across the island. I knew what I had to do there and then, with Peter in good spirits despite looking jaundiced and gaunt. 'Peter I have something to tell you.' He looked up, reading my face straight away. This was serious, not just a bit of shared gossip. 'There's no easy way to say this. You and me have a son'. I gulped out the words, swallowing hard. There, done it. Said it. His eyes widened, a mix of confusion and something else. Fear? Shock? It was hard to tell. He didn't answer, so I filled the void talking way too quickly. My teenage pregnancy, running away to Cornwall, keeping everything not just from him but from my family, St Brigid's, adoption and only recently, the reunion between mother and son. His eyes changed. What now? I still couldn't tell but there were tears forming, a catch of the throat. Then his questions came thick and fast, his voice now angry and accusatory. Why had I hidden it from him? What possessed me to live a lie for so long? Then there were the ones about Andy. Did he know I was in touch with his birth father? How could I have met with him and lied yet again. On and on, until both of us were too exhausted to continue. We'll carry on the conversation tomorrow and some big decisions will need to be made. But the worst is

surely over – isn't it? '

Reading back my words, it's as if I'm right back in that bright room in Tenerife, the sun streaming in and the sea sparkling in the distance. Peter propped up in bed, sobbing and finally asking me to leave him alone to collect his thoughts. Afterwards, I went out to sit in the garden and didn't move for several hours. When Lulu, Kevin and Amy returned, all of them in high spirits from their trip out, they realised straight away something was wrong.

'Is everything all right Debbie, dad OK?' Lulu asked, looking concerned.

'You'll have to talk to him' I replied distractedly, while Amy and Kevin exchanged looks. I'd already told them that I was going to tell Peter the truth at some point but they hadn't realised that I'd planned it for that very day. Now they knew all right and after Lulu disappeared to find her dad, we all just sat there, no-one wanting to speak.

It was Kevin who finally broke the silence.

'Look let's get out of here for tonight, go and book into a hotel. If you've just done what I think you have, they'll need some space.'

That's exactly what we did but not before Lulu barged out to tell us that it was probably best if we left for now. She looked pale, stunned and kept staring hard at me. If she was thinking 'you lying hurtful bitch' she wasn't going to say so.

We quickly packed up our stuff and checked into a nearby hotel, remaining there only for a day but it felt much longer. Lulu then rang to say that Peter really wanted us to stay on the island for the rest of the week and that we should head back over to his house.

'He wants you all to come over this evening' she said, adding that he'd told her everything.

'Is he all right?' I asked, knowing the answer. Of course he wasn't, he'd just had some mind blowing news.

'He just needs time for it to sink in. We all do...' Lulu replied and I could hear the exhaustion in her voice. Pregnant, sick dad, and now this on top of everything else.

Then the first the big family summit. Peter dressed and sitting at the dinner table, Lulu with her Spanish husband Carlos and us three, sombre and not knowing what to expect. There was a large bottle of wine on the table, with a label that said 'expensive'.

Peter, looking frail but dapper, asked Lulu to uncork the wine and I was right. It was a vintage red, the sort only to be opened for a special occasion.

We all stayed silent as Lulu popped out the cork, letting Peter smell the wine before filling our glasses. She didn't ask us if we wanted any, it was assumed that we did.

'I bought this over ten years ago with no idea when and why I would open it. Today's the day though, and I want us all to make a toast. I'll have just one sip and then stick with the water.'

We all waited for Peter to propose the toast and then he turned directly to me.

'To Debbie, our son and all of our futures whatever that may be'

None of us could have foreseen this reaction but his message was clear. He wanted to meet Andy and involve him in his life.

....

Back to last year's diary, this time two months after the trip to Tenerife. By then, Peter and I had spoken at length about the best way to tell Andy. He agreed it had to be face-to-face, with me breaking the news first.

As things stood, that fitted in with Andy's plan to visit Truro. He didn't bring his fiancée Lauren with him, instead opting to visit alone.

I left it a few days to allow him to get to know Amy, explore Truro and the surrounding countryside. He loved Cornwall, marvelling at the architecture, the changing landscapes and the awe inspiring beaches. Amy and him bonded quickly, sharing the same sense of humour and love of Indie rock music.

Another extract from the diary. It was three days after Andy had arrived and the time just seemed right. We were on our own, Amy out with a friend and Kevin doing a late shift at work.

'Well diary. I've finally told Andy everything too and

like Peter, his first reaction was one of stunned silence. Then he hugged me, telling me not to keep apologising for lying about his real dad. After all, I'd done what I thought was best and that was good enough for him. As he said this, the emotion finally got the better of me and it took a while to compose myself. There he was, being so damned sweet, not a trace of anger or resentment. God knows those parents of his have done an amazing job bless them both. We haven't called Peter tonight but Andy wants to do it tomorrow, first thing. Then he'll tell his parents and Lauren. Just before he went to bed he told me that he loved me – the first time he has said it. He then added that 'none of this will come as a surprise to Lauren' and of course, I understood what he meant by that. I don't mind admitting that as I write this I'm in bits, relieved but happy.'

....

When father and son did get to speak, it was faltering at first, each being careful not to tread on the feelings of the other. The conversation with Andy's parents and fiancée was much more fraught, with Lauren telling Andy that she 'told him so.' She'd spotted from the beginning that I hadn't been telling the whole story and for that she can most certainly take credit. I can only now hope that she too will forgive me but it's something still to be sorted out.

As for my mum and sister in Wales, that's a work in progress. At first my sister Carol refused to speak to me, telling me that the news 'could kill mum' and that I was a conniving, selfish bitch. I wrote a letter explaining why I did what I did but it went unanswered. I then wrote again saying that I'd come to Wales but got a curt answer message to say 'don't bother, just leave us alone'.

I was still going to head across there anyway, when out of the blue Carol turned up on the doorstep. More tears, shouting and recriminations but at the end of it, we agreed an uneasy truce. We are in touch but that's just about it and time may well yet prove to be a healer. Neither mum nor Carol has met Andy or Peter's family but I hope one day that they will.

Father and son finally got to meet up a just few weeks ago. Andy travelled to Tenerife for a private visit, this time with fiancée Lauren, and by all accounts things have gone well. When he's in better health, Peter will make a trip over to Toronto and his medically trained adopted son, the one and only 'Dr Andrew Wilson', is already dispensing some good health advice to his birth dad.

As for the relationship between me and Peter, well let's see. The forgiveness is already there and that's the best I can hope for.

And what do Andy's parents, Theresa and Joe, make of all of this? I've spoken to them and like Andy, there has been no blame or accusations, just acceptance. Last time I spoke to Theresa she was more concerned about my welfare, which is so typical of her. I'll say it once again and will keep on saying it thorough my life. Andy couldn't have had better parents if I'd picked them myself.

Now that the whole truth is out, I've made a few resolutions for this brand new year.

The first is to get us all together, our complicated and newly blended family, to mark the beginning of our connected lives. I'm not sure when that will be but perhaps the future wedding of Andy and Lauren could be the catalyst – assuming that Lauren is a willing partner of course.

The next is to pay greater attention to my lovely partner, Kevin, who has been so supportive through all of this, never once complaining or feeling sorry for himself. Time now to concentrate on 'us' as a couple and do that trip to New York that we promised ourselves all those months ago. Just go more carefully on that damned scooter this time Kevin.

Then there is Philippe Roux, the kindly stranger I met in Toronto, who is now a friend and has been a great source of advice over the past year. Whatever else happens, I've resolved to keep stay touch with him and have grown to view him as a sort of kindly 'guardian angel', like Clarence in one of my favourite films, 'It's A Wonderful Life.' Monsieur Roux, a calm presence in an often stormy world.

Oh and just one more resolution.

I know the 'old Debbie' never wanted to look back, but I can't help wondering what really did happen to my teenage best friend, Charlie? Now there's a bit of detective work that will finally tie up all the loose ends from my past.

And that folks really is it. Time to file away last year's diary and start afresh.

Here's to a new year, a clean life slate and to my extended family. Each and every one of them this time round

Review.

Now that you have read this novella, would you consider writing a review? Reviews are the best way for readers to discover new books and will be much appreciated.

And if you enjoyed this series of Dilemma Novellas then do try the novel 'My Bermuda Namesakes', or my short story 'Key' . See details and reviews on websites www.maggiefogarty.com and www.amazon.co.uk/www.amazon.com.

About the Author:

Maggie Fogarty is a Royal Television Society award winning television producer and journalist, making TV programmes for all the major UK broadcasters. She has also written extensively for a number of national newspapers and magazines.

In April 2011 her story 'Namesakes' was a finalist in the Writers and Artists/WAYB short story competition.

'My Bermuda Namesakes' was her debut novel and grew out of the original short story. It was written during a year long stay in Bermuda where Maggie's husband, Paul, was working as a digital forensics consultant. During her time on the island, Maggie wrote a guest column for the Bermuda Sun newspaper.

'Backwards and Forwards' is Maggie's third novella and forms part of a trilogy called the 'Dilemma Novellas'.

Maggie and her husband now live Cornwall in the far South West of England with their cockapoo dog Bonnie. Before moving there, they lived on the outskirts of Birmingham, in the English Midlands, where Maggie was born and grew up.

Author website: www.maggiefogarty.com

32015442R00081

Printed in Great Britain
by Amazon